Thanks!

Dealing with Denver

Carolynn Carey

In memory of Tony Evans, who exemplified
all of the best qualities of humankind.
Selfless, and with a love of life
that endeared him to everyone
who knew him, Tony's sacrifices
for his country, his love
for his family, and
his contributions
to his community
will live on
and on.

1947-2009

Dealing with Denver

Carolynn Carey

ISBN-13: 978-1-4486-4048-5
ISBN-10: 1-4486-4048-2

This book is a work of fiction. Names, characters, places, and incidents are either products of the author's imagination or used fictitiously. Any similarity to actual persons, living or dead, organizations, and/or events is purely coincidental.

Trademarks Acknowledgements

The author acknowledges the trademark status and trademark owners of the following wordmarks mentioned in this work of fiction:

Mercedes: Daimler AG
Toyota: TA Toyota Motor Corporation

About the Author

Carolynn Carey is the award-winning author of three books. The first two, *A Summer Sentence* and *Falling for Dallas,* are set in Barbourville, Tennessee, as is this book.

Carolynn was born and raised in a small town in Tennessee, and while none of the characters in this book are based on people she knew there, the camaraderie and closeness of small-town life are certainly drawn from her experiences.

While Carolynn now lives in a city, she enjoys visiting the fictional Barbourville from time to time and hopes you will also enjoy the trip.

If you'd like to know more about Carolynn and her books, visit her web site at www.CarolynnCarey.com.

About Raynaud's Disease

I remember from my teenage years seeing my father coming through the front door on a winter's evening and holding his hands up to show us fingers that were as white as the snow outside. We had no idea that it was a condition with a name. I had almost forgotten those occasions when, as an adult, I experienced my first episode of the strange malady. Curious, I researched the condition and learned that it is known as Raynaud's Disease. Since that time, I've met several people who suffer from Raynaud's Disease. For most, it is just a nuisance, but for others, it can present a real problem. If you want to know more about Raynaud's, a great deal of information is available on the Internet.

—Carolynn Carey

THE PEOPLE OF BARBOURVILLE AND McCRAY COUNTY

Mattie Meadows - A freelance writer who is visiting Barbourville to write an article on Potter Place for a magazine about cottage vacation spots.

Denver Vance - An attorney who stops en route to his home in Chicago to visit his brother, Dallas, in Barbourville.

Dallas Vance - One of the Vance triplets, he moved from Chicago, married a Barbourville native, and owns Potter Place.

Beth Ann Stanfield Vance - Dallas' wife and the mother of Trevor Stanfield and Matthew Vance.

Megan Marsh McCray - Niece of Denver and Dallas, wife of Daniel McCray, and mother of triplet girls.

Daniel McCray - Sheriff of McCray County.

Bill McCray - Daniel's father and mayor of Barbourville, Tennessee. His brothers are Josh, Richard, and Bob.

Josh McCray - An attorney in Barbourville and brother to Bill, Richard, and Bob McCray.

Richard McCray - An architect in Barbourville and brother to Bill, Josh, and Bob McCray.

Bob McCray - The McCray County judge and brother to Bill, Josh, and Richard McCray.

Evelyn McCray - Wife of Judge Bob McCray.

Eloise Smithfield - Josh's partner and friend.

Lily Martin - Town librarian and Richard's friend.

One

Mattie Meadows settled back in the wooden porch swing and, with a fond smile, listened to the song of a night bird trilling from somewhere in the front yard of the Potter cottage. Was this a detail she should include in her article? Maybe, depending on what other particulars she noted tonight.

Taking note of details was, after all, part of her job. And in order to write an accurate magazine article about Potter Place, she had to experience its ambiance at all times of the day, including the late evening. She closed her eyes and prepared to soak up the atmosphere, paying particular attention to the sounds, the air temperature, even the quality of the darkness at this hour of the evening.

"Eleven o'clock and all is well," she murmured to herself. Still, while it was true that she felt entirely safe sitting outside alone in a residential section of the small town of

Barbourville, Tennessee, she believed in being cautious. Her cell phone lay in the seat beside her, and she had programmed it with the local sheriff's telephone number.

Not that she thought she'd need to call the sheriff, not in Barbourville where the most recent criminal activity probably consisted of a case of jaywalking. Still, she'd learned in her travels not to take anything for granted, which meant she should really get to work so she could finish up here and return to the comfort and security of her nice, cozy room in Dunmore's Bed and Breakfast south of town.

Mr. and Mrs. Dunmore ran a delightful B and B, and Mattie was enjoying her stay there. An unexpected bonus, she had soon discovered, was that Mrs. Dunmore was equal to a town crier, which was especially helpful to Mattie in her line of work. As soon as Carmen Dunmore had learned that Mattie planned to write a magazine article about Potter Place, she'd launched into a detailed history of the cottage, including the fact that it was now owned by Dallas Vance, who had moved to Barbourville from Chicago and ended up married to the cottage's previous owner.

Dallas Vance, Mrs. Dunmore had continued, was one of a set of triplet brothers, and they looked so much alike that it was nearly impossible to tell them apart. But that was rarely a problem for the folk of Barbourville because the other brothers, Denver and Dayton, still lived in Chicago where they continued to work in the family law firm.

Mattie had talked with Dallas on the phone when she'd obtained his permission to write about the cottage for *Cot-*

tage Vacations, but she hadn't actually met him until earlier in the week when she'd gotten together with him and his wife. She'd been impressed with the friendliness of Dallas and Beth Ann, who made a strikingly attractive couple, Beth Ann with her red hair and alabaster complexion and Dallas with his dark hair and square jaw. They'd offered to let Mattie stay in the cottage while she researched it, but she'd explained that she preferred to live off the premises when she wrote about a dwelling to ensure that she could be totally impartial.

Now, some five days later, she wished she could have taken them up on the offer. The cottage was a charming place, and she would heartily recommend it to the readers of *Cottage Vacations* as a rental destination.

In the meantime, however, she needed to finish recording her impressions of the cottage's atmosphere at night. She lifted her voice-activated recorder, held it close to her lips, and began dictating a portion of her article.

"In late evening in the early spring, if you've a mind to, you can relax in the wooden swing on the front porch of Potter Place and revel in the joys of the cool, crisp mountain air and almost total darkness.

"Note to self: Omit the word cool—it's redundant."

She continued: "If you're fortunate, a soft breeze will gift you with the heady fragrance wafting from either of the massive lilac bushes growing at each end of the porch. The silence is almost complete except for the occasional call of a night bird and the rare sound of a vehicle—

"Whoa! What's that?" She lowered her recorder and stood as a car turned the corner at the end of the block. The lone streetlight at the corner illuminated the vehicle for only a second, but its headlights were an unwelcome intrusion that momentarily blinded Mattie.

She grabbed her cell phone and opened it, prepared to press the button for Sheriff McCray if she thought it was necessary. But first she hurried to stand in front of the screen door. She had opened the cottage up earlier, and she could easily step inside and lock the door behind her if she felt threatened.

She felt a tad silly, being so cautious. The vehicle probably belonged to one of the neighborhood teenagers just getting in from a Saturday night date and no doubt it would glide right on past.

But no, the car coasted up to the curb in front of the cottage. Dallas and Beth Ann had assured Mattie that she would have full access to Potter Place both day and night because they didn't plan to rent it for the next few weeks.

Which meant that whoever was driving that car had no business being there, and Mattie intended to tell him or her to move on just as soon as her unwanted visitor stepped out onto the street.

* * *

Denver Vance cut the motor of his car, unfastened his seat belt, and rolled his tired shoulders. Now that he had arrived, he had to admit that he should have kept to his original plan and spent the night in Atlanta.

That's what he'd told everyone he planned to do—leave his conference in Florida that morning, spend the night in Atlanta, and drive on to Barbourville the following day.

But when he'd arrived in Atlanta, he hadn't wanted to stop and spend the night in an impersonal hotel. Not when he had relatives in Barbourville, both with delightful Victorian houses featuring plenty of room.

In addition to his brother, Denver also had a niece living in Barbourville. Megan was the daughter of Denver's sister, who had died when he and his brothers were just twelve years old. Now married to the local sheriff and with triplet daughters of her own, Megan still adored her doting uncles and would have welcomed having Denver stay with her.

Unfortunately, Denver had underestimated the time it would take him to drive from Atlanta to Barbourville. He'd figured the mileage as though the entire route was made up of interstate, forgetting that the last sixty miles was a winding country road where he couldn't make more than thirty-five miles an hour.

Then he arrived in Barbourville to find both Dallas' and Megan's houses completely dark, meaning everyone he knew was probably already asleep. He'd decided to spend the night in Dallas' cottage instead of disturbing either household.

After all, Dallas had long ago given him his own key to the cottage and had recently explained that he wouldn't be renting the place for a few weeks because he and Beth Ann were just too busy to deal with renters, what with caring for little Matthew and with the upsurge in Dallas' renovation and resell business.

Denver knew Beth Ann always kept fresh sheets on the cottage's beds, and that's all he required for the night. In the morning he would walk across the back yard to his brother's house and announce his presence.

He got out of the car, stood for a few seconds breathing deep of the cool mountain air, then stepped around to the back of the car to open his trunk. He pulled out a duffel bag and set it on the pavement, then reached for his shaving kit. He looked up quickly when a disembodied voice called to him from somewhere in the darkness.

"I would suggest that you not get anything else out of that trunk, mister."

It was a female's voice, but that was about all he could tell. He glanced around. A streetlight at the far corner shed a tiny bit of light on the street around him, but the surrounding yards were completely black.

He spoke into the darkness. "Where are you?"

"I'm where I'm supposed to be. Where do you think you're going with that luggage?"

Denver frowned. He didn't care for the female's attitude, but he was at a disadvantage, not being able to judge exactly where she was located. If he had to guess, he'd say her voice had come from the cottage porch, so he looked in that direction when he responded.

"My brother owns this cottage. I just got into town, and I was planning to spend the night here. He told me he didn't intend to rent it for a while." He stepped up onto the sidewalk. His eyes had adjusted to the darkness and he was almost certain he could make out a form standing on the porch. "Did Dallas change his mind and rent the cottage to you?"

"How do I know you're Dallas Vance's brother?"

Denver was now certain the voice originated from the cottage porch. "Turn the light on and look at me. If you've seen Dallas, you'll know I'm his brother."

His suggestion was followed by silence. Denver had begun to suspect that the woman was a trespasser, possibly even someone who had broken into the cottage. He decided his safest course was to drive around to Redbud Road and inform Megan's husband, Sheriff Daniel McCray, about the situation. He placed his duffel bag back in the trunk, closed the lid, and started toward the front of his car.

"Where are you going?" the woman called to him.

Denver ignored her.

"Wait a minute." Screen door hinges screeched, followed by the click of a light switch. The bulb in the fixture on the porch ceiling came on, spilling light down the walk toward the street. "Okay, mister, the light's on now. Let me take a look at you."

Denver paused, then turned slowly. Since he intended to give Daniel a heads-up on this suspicious female, it would be good if he could provide a description of her.

She stood directly under the porch light, perfect for

his purposes. He stared at her, mentally cataloguing the features he would use to describe her to the sheriff.

Top to bottom, item one: Shiny blonde hair, pulled up into a curly ponytail, glistening in the light like dozens of flickering fireflies.

Denver gulped, downright horrified by the direction his thoughts had taken. Where had that bit about fireflies come from? He was an attorney, for heaven's sake, not a poet. Scratch the glistening and flickering part.

Item two. Large blue eyes. Really gorgeous blue eyes. Wait! He was doing it again. He reminded himself that her eyes were just eyes. Blue eyes. Nothing more.

Item three. Cute little nose. He gritted his teeth and took a deep breath. What was wrong with him? Oh well, no need to describe the nose. The sheriff would assume she had one.

Then the lips. Was he on item three or item four? It didn't matter because the lips were indescribable anyway. Full, curving, half-smiling, enticing. He couldn't think of any adjectives dealing with the lips that he could repeat to the sheriff.

Forget the face then. The clothing and other features were more critical for a description anyway.

Height: Maybe 5 foot, 8 inches, much of which could be attributed to exceptionally long, shapely legs encased in jeans that fit like a second skin. He smothered a groan. He'd better not try to describe the legs when he talked to Daniel. Instead he would simply pass along the estimated height.

Next would be her weight: Just right, obviously. Not too thin and not too heavy. Slender but with excellent curves.

He gave himself a mental kick. He needed to stay on track, to concentrate on features that could be of use to the sheriff. Okay. Clothes. In addition to the jeans, which were dark blue, she wore a long-sleeved tee, kind of a tan color, with a logo on the chest that he couldn't read from this distance. White running shoes. That was it.

The woman must have decided he'd stared long enough. She propped her hands on her hips. "If you're through inspecting me, why don't you step up here where I can get a better look at you?"

Denver walked slowly up the sidewalk, not taking his eyes off the female. A slight frown pulled at her brow, and as he came closer, she took a quick step back toward the screen door, as though preparing to duck inside if she felt threatened.

Denver paused at the bottom of the concrete steps leading up to the porch and gazed at the woman, allowing the overhead light to illuminate his features.

She cocked her head to one side. "Well, I have to admit that you look exactly like Dallas Vance. Obviously you're his brother, so I guess it'll be okay if I leave you here for the night."

Denver frowned. "What do you mean, leave me here for the night? Who are you anyway?"

She stepped to the edge of the porch and stuck her hand out, a gesture so brisk and so unexpected that Denver didn't realize for a second that she intended to shake hands. If he was a little slow responding, she didn't seem to notice. She just continued to hold her hand out. "I'm Matilda Meadows. My friends call me Mattie."

Denver took her hand and immediately realized he liked the feel of it. Although her hand was much smaller than his, her handshake was firm. He was sorry when she broke the contact, but he certainly wasn't prepared to leave a stranger on his brother's front porch without more of an explanation from her. "Hi Mattie. I'm Denver. I don't mean to sound rude, but since Dallas and Beth Ann aren't renting the cottage for a while, what are you doing here?"

She smiled. "It's simple, really. I'm a freelance writer and I have an assignment from *Cottage Vacations* to write a magazine article about this place. Dallas agreed and has given me full access to the cottage for a few days. I was just sitting on the porch trying to soak up some atmosphere. I prefer to get to know a structure during all periods of the day and night before I write it up."

"So you're staying in the cottage while you're here?"

"No. Dallas offered but I turned him down. I don't like to feel indebted to the people I'm writing about. I'm staying at Dunmore's Bed and Breakfast south of town, so you're free to spend the night here. I'm sorry about my initial suspicions, but I was under the impression that the cottage would be vacant while I was in town. I wish Dallas had warned me that you might be staying here."

"He didn't know. I'd told him I was spending the night in Atlanta. When I changed my mind, I didn't bother to call because I expected to be in town much earlier than this. The drive took a lot longer than I thought it would."

She nodded. "I ran into the same thing when I drove up here. Look, I started a pot of decaf coffee before I came out on the porch. If you don't mind, I'll fix myself a cup to go and then I'll get out of your way."

To his surprise, Denver discovered he wasn't in any hurry for her to leave. "Why don't you go ahead and drink your coffee here? In fact, if you've got enough to spare a cup, I'll join you."

She smiled. "There's plenty, and I'd love to have you join me. If you want to be carrying your luggage inside, I'll pour both of us a cup of coffee and let you know when it's ready."

"Okay." Denver waited until Mattie stepped inside the cottage before he turned and walked back to his car. He was glad the woman had a good reason for being at the cottage. Of course, she could be lying, but he didn't think so, and he considered himself a good judge of character.

Five minutes later, he had unloaded his duffel bag, shaving kit, and clothing bag. He set everything in the foyer and went back for his laptop and the sport coat he'd worn this morning during the last session of the conference.

Back inside again, he placed his laptop on the small table in the foyer and draped his coat over the back of a straight chair sitting beside the table.

Mattie stepped into the foyer. "The coffee's ready."

Denver looked at her and smiled. She really was one of the most attractive women he'd ever seen. "Thanks! Lead the way."

As he started to follow Mattie, he brushed against the chair where he'd hung his sport coat. The chair fell over with a clatter.

Mattie spun around, then let her breath out in a quick sigh. "You startled me."

"Sorry." He bent to pick the chair up while Mattie rescued his sport coat from the floor. As she lifted it, she suddenly stilled, staring at the lapel.

Denver set the chair upright, then reached for his coat but paused when Mattie lifted it close to her face. "What's this?" she asked.

Denver glanced at the object that had attracted her attention. "Oh, I guess I forgot to take my name tag off after I left the conference. Is something wrong?"

Her eyes widened. "You just came from a conference for private investigators?"

"Yes, but I didn't choose this particular conference because of the private investigation portion. All of the sessions I attended were designed for people with an interest in electronics."

Mattie frowned. "I thought you were an attorney."

"I am, but I enjoy electronics as a hobby. One of my buddies owns his own security and electronics business and I help him out sometimes. I attended the conference hoping to pick up some pointers for the security portion of his business."

"A security business?" She was still frowning as though totally confused.

"Alarm systems, that type of thing."

Her frown faded. "But you do know a little about private investigation techniques, right?"

"Not much. Why?"

She shrugged. "Nothing important. Let's go have that coffee."

She turned quickly but not before Denver noted the corners of her lips turning up in a small smile. Her reaction to his name tag was puzzling. All the more reason to take the time to get to know her, he decided, trailing her toward the kitchen. If she wasn't on the up-and-up, he'd want to warn his brother and the sheriff.

But the most important reason for getting to know her better, he admitted, was because he'd never experienced such instant attraction to a female before, and by becoming better acquainted with her, he hoped to find out whether the feeling was a temporary aberration or something more.

Two

Probably the last thing she needed tonight was a cup of coffee, even if it *was* decaf, Mattie concluded, walking ahead of Denver toward the cottage's small kitchen. After all, her stomach already felt fluttery, a sensation she had long associated with nerves.

But why she'd be nervous was a mystery to her. Sure, Denver Vance was a good-looking man, just like his brother Dallas, with that same thick dark hair lying softly on his collar, those same clear blue eyes sparkling with intelligence and wit, that same square chin that surely could be indicative of a stubborn streak.

So what? Mattie had seen her share of handsome men over the years, but she had never felt this sort of jittery anticipation before. No doubt her reactions could be explained by the question she intended to ask him as soon as the opportunity presented itself.

She stepped into the kitchen and walked to the counter

where the drip coffee maker was located. She picked up the two cups of coffee she'd poured and carried them to the table where she'd already placed a plate of homemade cookies Beth Ann had sent over earlier in the day.

Denver had paused when he stepped into the room. A smile touched his lips as he looked around. "Nice," he murmured, glancing at the colorful sun-catcher in the window and then at the large pottery jug sitting in the corner. "Every time I visit, I see something new Beth Ann has added." Then his gaze cut to the cookies and his smile broadened. "A late-night snack is just what I need. And that coffee sure smells good. Thanks for letting me join you."

Mattie returned his smile. "You're most welcome. I couldn't drink an entire pot of coffee by myself anyway. Have a seat."

Suddenly aware that Denver was waiting on her to be seated first, she pulled out her chair and sat down. She wasn't accustomed in this day and age to men paying much attention to such niceties. He must have had a good upbringing, she decided.

She pushed the pink Depression glass sugar bowl and creamer across the table toward him. She'd found them in the cabinet and been amazed that the cottage came furnished with a complete set of valuable dishes in the Cabbage Rose pattern. "I hope you don't mind flavored cream. It's one of my indulgences, and I stopped today at the supermarket so I could stock the refrigerator here."

"Thanks anyway, but I drink mine black." Denver helped himself to a chocolate chip cookie. "This looks homemade."

"You can thank your sister-in-law for those. She sent them over this afternoon. She seems very nice."

"Yeah, Dallas lucked up getting Beth Ann to marry him. Have you met her son?"

"Which one?"

Denver grimaced. "I keep forgetting about the baby although I don't know how I could. Dallas talks about little Matthew constantly. But actually, I was referring to Trevor."

Mattie grinned, remembering the handsome young man who'd brought the cookies to her. "He's a charmer. I understand his father, Beth Ann's first husband, was killed in a car wreck."

"Yeah, from what I hear, that happened before Trevor was even born. Beth Ann had it rough for a long time trying to raise a son on her own, but she did a great job of it."

Mattie set her teeth. Thoughts of a single woman raising a child on her own reminded her of one of the reasons she'd gone out of her way to get an assignment in Barbourville.

And it was almost as though the gods had dropped Denver Vance right into her lap to help her.

But how to ask the question?

She picked up the cream pitcher and poured a healthy

dollop into her coffee, then reached for a cookie and carefully centered it on her pretty pink plate.

"So, what did you learn about security at the conference you attended?" She had tried to keep the tone of her question casual but was afraid she'd sounded a little too intense when Denver's gaze cut to her fairly quickly.

But perhaps she'd just imagined that. He smiled and shrugged. "I learned that the technology is advancing almost too fast for me to keep up with it, but I picked up lots of brochures to take back to Steve."

"Steve's your friend?"

"Right." Denver reached for a second cookie, then paused with his hand over the plate. "Am I going to run you low on cookies?"

"Please, eat all you want. I've had too many of them today as it is." She'd only had one, but she didn't intend to mention that. If chocolate chip cookies would keep Denver occupied while she beat around the bush trying to lead up to what she wanted to ask him, he could have the entire plate.

"Why didn't Steve go to the conference himself?"

A tiny frown touched Denver's brow, as though he'd forgotten what they were talking about and had to think back for a second before answering. "Oh, well, Steve couldn't get away from the business, and actually, I didn't really have time myself. The law firm is pretty busy right now, but my brother Dayton insisted that I take a vacation, and the conference appealed to me because it took place in a warm climate and because I could expand my knowledge about security systems."

"I can understand your reasons for wanting to go, but why would your brother insist you take a vacation at this time of year?"

Denver took a swallow of his coffee and then nodded toward the coffee carafe sitting on the counter. "Do you mind if I get a refill?"

"Help yourself, please." She paused while Denver poured his coffee. As soon as he sat back down, she spoke again. "You were about to tell me why your brother wanted you to go on a vacation now."

Denver smiled. "You must have a background in investigative reporting. You're relentless."

Mattie's mouth went dry. She hoped she hadn't alienated Denver. She needed an ally in this town, and he was the best bet she'd seen so far. She lowered her gaze. "Sorry. I do tend to be a bit too pushy sometimes. At least that's what my mother says."

"Don't apologize. I was mostly kidding. Besides, it's not a deep, dark secret. Dayton says I work too much just because I haven't taken a vacation in three years." He paused and sighed. "But mostly I agreed because of my flooded house."

Mattie frowned. "Your house was flooded? What happened?"

"The water filter under my kitchen sink burst, and unfortunately, it happened on a Saturday morning after I'd left to help Steve with one of his projects. When I got home that afternoon, water was an inch deep all over the house."

"That must have been a mess."

"Dayton said it was a blessing in disguise because I'd been meaning to do some renovations anyway. So Dayton, being Dayton, suggested in the strongest terms that I go on vacation while turning my house over to a contractor to repair the floors, do some rewiring, and get the place ready for me to move back into. I decided to go to the conference to help pass part of the three weeks I need to be out of my house."

Mattie had to bite back a smile of happiness. She'd just learned that Denver could spend a little more time in Barbourville if he wanted to. But she couldn't afford to approach her topic too quickly. Instead she asked, "What did you mean when you said 'Dayton, being Dayton'?"

Denver grinned. "Dayton was born a few minutes earlier than me or Dallas so he considers himself the eldest and has always tried to boss us around. Dallas usually ignores him, but I go along most of time, at least when it suits me. This time it suited me to use some of my vacation time because I had to vacate the house for a while anyway."

"You live alone then?" Mattie had already noticed that Denver wasn't wearing a wedding ring but that didn't mean he didn't have house mates.

"Yep, I've lived alone ever since I graduated from college. Dallas bought himself a condo near downtown, which didn't suit me, and Dayton stayed in the home place when Mom and Dad moved to Arizona. I wanted something different, so I bought a place in one of the older neighborhoods. I like the house, but Dayton was right—it really did need some work done on it, and I'd never gotten around to having it done. But we've talked enough about me. What about you? Where are you from?"

Mattie lifted her cup and took another sip of coffee to give herself time to think. Subtlety was called for and she wasn't quite sure which part of her story to tell first. She picked up the sugar bowl and gazed at it for a second before recalling that she didn't take sugar in her coffee. She set it back down and met Denver's gaze, which had grown a bit puzzled.

"I'm adopted," she said. So much for subtlety. She blew her breath out in a quick sigh. "By really wonderful people," she continued. "My adoptive parents were told they couldn't have children, so they adopted me. Then they had a boy and a girl of their own."

Denver nodded but the slight frown pulling at his forehead suggested he hadn't really expected so much detail so quickly. "Having two children of their own must have come as a surprise to your parents."

"Yes, indeed. They were thrilled, of course. And they always assured me that I was loved just as much as their natural children. And I knew I was. There was never a question in my mind."

Denver nodded again. "I heard an unspoken 'but' at the end of that sentence."

Mattie managed a smile although she knew it must appear a bit wan. "You're right. I want to find my birth mother."

"You sound very determined."

Mattie shut her eyes. She was handling this badly, probably portraying herself as more obsessed than determined. But maybe that was accurate. Perhaps she was obsessed. Which probably meant she should share only the most superficial of her reasons.

She opened her eyes again. "The thing is, I've noticed over the years the rather amazing ways in which genetics plays a part in a person's physical makeup. For example, Dad and my sister Shelley have a little mole in exactly the same spot on their necks, and both Mom and my brother Blake have long, narrow feet. If such small features can be inherited, what about the big things? What about genetic abnormalities? If I'm ever to have children of my own, I want to know what they might inherit from me. I want to know who my parents were."

Denver nodded. "I can understand that. I assume you've tried to find your mother."

"Yes, I've been working on it for the last couple of years, and I think I may have a very good lead now. The thing is, she apparently doesn't want to be found, and I don't know how to reach her and convince her that I have no desire to cause an upheaval in her life. All I want is a medical background. Then, if she wants me to disappear forever, I'm perfectly willing to do so."

"That makes sense." Denver turned his cup up and drained it. "I wish you the best in locating her." He pushed his chair back.

Suddenly aware that time was running out, Mattie reached across the table and grabbed his wrist. "Wait. I want to ask you something."

Denver's gaze dropped to her hand. Then he did the most surprising thing. He gently but firmly twisted his arm until he could grasp her hand, holding on to her in a way she found amazingly warm and comforting.

He gave her hand an encouraging squeeze. "You sound a little upset. What is it you want to ask me?"

Mattie moistened her lips, which had suddenly gone dry. When she spoke, her voice sounded strange in her own ears, strained and almost whispery. She hadn't realized quite how important this was to her until she was about to verbalize her need. She took a deep breath and looked directly into Denver's eyes. "I'm almost positive my birth mother lives here in Barbourville. I want you to help me locate her."

Three

Denver gradually released his grasp on Mattie's hand. He'd enjoyed visiting with her over coffee and cookies. In fact, he could hardly believe he'd opened up so much, told her so many things about himself. He rarely discussed his personal life, especially with someone he'd just met.

But there was something about Mattie that made him feel at ease, as though they were old friends. He really wished he could help her search for her birth mother. He would enjoy spending more time with her. But for her sake, he had to tell her the truth.

"You don't want my help, Mattie. I'm almost as much a stranger here as you are. A lot of people in Barbourville know who I am, of course, because they're acquainted with Dallas, and they seem to adore my niece, who married the local sheriff. But they don't have any reason to trust me or answer any questions I might ask them. You need to talk to

Megan's husband. As sheriff, Daniel probably knows just about everybody in the entire county."

Mattie shook her head. "I can't do that."

"Why not?"

"I have reason to believe my mother may be related to Sheriff McCray in some way."

Denver frowned in concentration, trying to recall what he had heard about Daniel McCray's family. He knew the McCrays had been around for a lot of years. After all, the county was named after them.

And they were still influential people. Daniel's father was the mayor of Barbourville, the county seat, and his Uncle Bob was the county judge. Two other uncles, an architect and an attorney, were prominent members of the community, and even Daniel's mother had a lot of clout in Barbourville. Her maiden name had been Barbour.

Finally he shook his head. "What little I know about the McCrays isn't going to help you. I know that Daniel is an only child, and I'm pretty sure he doesn't have any aunts on his father's side of the family. I'm not sure about his mother's people."

"It wouldn't be on the Barbour side," Mattie said. She picked up her cup of coffee, then set it back down. "At least from what I've learned, the name of McCray definitely was involved."

"Couldn't you just go to the sheriff and ask outright what he knows?"

Mattie sighed. "I may try that as a last resort, but I'd prefer not to alert the McCrays as to my purpose. If my existence is a secret that they are determined to keep hidden, they might try to cover up even more intensely if they know I'm actively searching."

Denver fiddled with his coffee cup. He had noticed as soon as Mattie sat down across the table from him that the small logo on her tee shirt read "Cottage Vacations: A Simpler Way." The words lay atop a graphic of an open magazine. He allowed his gaze to return to the logo. "Are you really writing a story about this cottage?"

He watched carefully as spots of color bloomed on her cheeks, and her eyes darkened when she met his gaze. "I certainly am. I'm not here under false pretenses if that's what you're thinking."

"No need to get upset. I'm not accusing you of underhanded tactics, but I had to ask. It's a bit of a coincidence, you getting an assignment in the town where you think your mother may be living."

Mattie grimaced. "Sorry! You're right. And it isn't a coincidence. I asked for the assignment because a friend told me about the cottage. She and her husband had stayed here last year and she thought *Cottage Vacations* would be interested in running an article about Potter Place. When I realized the cottage my friend was praising so highly was located in the town I'd just connected to my mother, I went to the editor and made a pitch, so here I am."

"Have you written articles for this particular magazine before?"

"Several times. I love cottages, particularly authentic ones like Potter Place. And believe me, Dallas checked my credentials thoroughly before he agreed to let me set foot in here. It's obvious that he loves this place."

"He put a lot of work into renovating the cottage, but he enjoyed it too. That's why he's buying several old houses in the county, renovating them, and reselling them. He feels that in addition to making a living, he's helping preserve some fine old architecture."

Mattie reached with both hands to massage the back of her neck. "Wow! All of sudden, I'm exhausted. I'm going to head back to the B and B."

Denver glanced at his watch. "No wonder you're tired. It's almost one o'clock in the morning. Where's your car? I didn't see one out front."

"It's parked across the street." She pushed back her chair and stood. "I'll stack the dishes in the sink if you'll put the cookies away."

Denver also stood. "I'll take care of everything in here as soon as I make sure you get to the B and B safely."

She cocked her head to one side. "Maybe you didn't hear me. My car's just across the street. I can drive myself."

"That's fine, but I'm following you in my car to make sure you get there safely."

A small smile lifted the corners of her lips. "Thanks,

Denver, but Barbourville isn't exactly a high crime district. I'll be fine."

He met her gaze squarely. "I don't doubt that, but I'm following you anyway, and you're wasting time arguing about it."

She rolled her eyes toward the ceiling, but she also grinned. "Fine. Are you ready?"

"Ready." Denver reached into his pocket, pulled out his car keys, and dangled them in front of her.

"Let's go then."

Ten minutes later, he pulled his car to a stop beside Mattie's in the parking lot of Dunmore's Bed and Breakfast on the outskirts of town. He got out, opened her car door for her, and walked her to the door of the inn.

He didn't speak until she smiled and said good night but by that time, he'd figured out a way to see her again. "How about coming back to the cottage for breakfast in the morning?"

She paused with her hand on the doorknob. "Break-fast?"

"Yes, breakfast."

"What time?"

"Ten?"

"I'll be there."

She frowned slightly, as though a bit puzzled that he'd extended the invitation. Then she stepped inside and closed the door behind her.

Denver drove back to the cottage slowly, wondering why on earth he'd invited Mattie to breakfast when he had no idea where he could find breakfast food in a small town on a Sunday morning.

At eight thirty the following morning, Denver stood on his brother's back porch and held his breath, straining to hear any noises that might be coming from Dallas' kitchen. Denver didn't want to disrupt his brother's household on a calm Sunday morning, but he sure hoped either Dallas or Beth Ann would be up and about.

Ah! At last he heard a noise coming from the kitchen. He quickly raised his hand and tapped on the door facing. A second later the door was pulled open. His brother, wearing pajama bottoms, a white tee shirt, and a disgruntled expression, glared at him through the screen door.

"Denver? What are you doing here at this hour of the morning? I thought you were still in Atlanta."

Denver hated when Dallas affected an expression of superiority. "Well, guess what, my all-knowing brother. I'm not in Atlanta. I'm on your doorstep and I need food and lots of it."

Dallas' frown deepened. "You don't look that hungry to me."

"It's not for me, dense one. It's for the woman I've invited to have breakfast with me at your cottage."

"Have you been drinking, Denver?"

Dealing with Denver

"Do you have any food or not? If you don't, at least tell me where I can find a grocery store open at this hour on a Sunday morning."

A female's voice sounded from behind Dallas. "Did I hear someone inquiring about food?"

A second later, Beth Ann Stanfield Vance pushed her body between her husband and the screen door. Dressed in jeans and a tee shirt with her red hair pulled back in a ponytail, she didn't look old enough to be little Matthew's mother, let alone the mother of a fourteen-year-old son by her first husband. She unlatched the screen. "Denver, honey, I'm so glad to see you. I wasn't expecting you this early but I'm delighted you're here. Come in."

Denver glared at his brother until Dallas finally took a step back and made room for him to come inside. He glanced around the bright kitchen and immediately found the sight he'd hoped for. Matthew, his only nephew, was seated in a high chair surrounded by half a dozen soft toys.

"Hey, big guy!" Denver hurried over to Matthew's side. Reaching out a hand, he used one finger to gently touch the soft down on the baby's head. "Are your Mama and Daddy treating you okay?"

Dallas pulled a chair out from the kitchen table and dropped into it. "Do you think he's grown since the last time you saw him?"

"You mean since last week? Yeah, I'd say so. He definitely looks bigger to me."

"I agree. He's going to be tall like his daddy."

"And like his uncle Denver too."

"Yeah, yeah. What are you doing here?"

"I told you. I need food."

Beth Ann, who'd been standing back and shaking her head at the brothers' banter, instantly stepped forward. "Oh sweetie, are you hungry?"

"No. I need food to take back to the cottage with me. I'm having company for breakfast."

Beth Ann's eyes widened. "Back to the cottage? Company? What am I missing?"

"I wouldn't mind knowing that myself," Dallas interjected.

Denver quickly explained how he'd gotten into town late the evening before and run into Mattie at the cottage. "Good thing she wasn't spending the night there," he told his brother, "or I'd have been waking you up at midnight."

"Your nephew does that often enough. I guess I could have tolerated you waking me up too."

Denver grinned. He and Dallas had always enjoyed picking at each other. It was how they showed their mutual affection. "I wouldn't have minded waking you up, but I didn't want to disturb Beth Ann or the baby or Trevor." He turned to Beth Ann. "Speaking of Trevor, where is that young man?"

Beth Ann heaved a sigh. "He's a teenager now, Denver. That means there's no way on earth he'd be out of bed this early on a Sunday morning."

"Of course. What was I thinking? I'll see him later then. I think I'll be staying a few days in the cottage if you folks don't mind."

Both Dallas and Beth Ann stared at him. "Staying?" Beth Ann said.

"For a few days?" Dallas chimed in.

Denver lifted his chin. "Hey, if you don't want me, just say so, okay?"

"No, no, sweetie." Beth Ann stepped to his side and gave him a quick hug. "We definitely want you to stay. It's just that…"

"What?"

Dallas pulled his brows down in a puzzled frown. "It's just that you're usually in a mad rush to get back to your routine in Chicago."

"Oh! Well, maybe so, but have you forgotten that my house was flooded? I can't go home again. Literally."

"I know about your house, Denver," Dallas said. "But I still expected you to rush back to Chicago and move in with Dayton until your house is ready. In fact, I distinctly remember you mentioning that as a possibility when you stopped by here last week on your way south."

"I decided I'd rather stay in the cottage a few days. Is that so hard to understand?"

"Yes," Dallas said.

"No, of course not, sweetie." Beth Ann glared at her husband for a second, then smiled at Denver. "Stay as long as you want. We're not renting the cottage through the summer months. Now what's this about you needing food? You're having a guest, did you say?"

Denver nodded. "I invited Mattie for breakfast, and she agreed to join me at ten this morning. Then I remembered that the cottage refrigerator is empty except for some cream Mattie bought for her coffee. Do you have any breakfast food I can borrow?"

"Certainly. I'll mix up a breakfast casserole that I can bake for you. That, along with some cheese grits and scratch biscuits should do it."

"Cheese grits?" Denver repeated, frowning. "Scratch biscuits?" He looked at Dallas and lifted his shoulders.

Dallas raised his brows. "Just go with it, Denver. It'll be great."

"If you say so, brother." He turned to his sister-in-law. "You're a lifesaver, Beth Ann. Thanks a million. You want me to come back in about an hour to pick up the food?"

"That'll be fine, Denver." Beth Ann sported a grin as she opened a cabinet door and pulled a box of grits off the shelf.

Four

When Mattie awoke on Sunday morning, she glanced around the strange room and wondered why she was feeling such a strong sense of anticipation.

Then she remembered.

She was going to Potter Place to have breakfast with Denver Vance.

A smile curved her lips while she stretched beneath the luxurious sheets, reveling in the warmth generated by the cotton blanket. The Dunmore's bed and breakfast was one of the nicest she'd ever patronized, and she was thrilled she had an excuse to remain in Barbourville a few more days. Hopefully Denver would hang around a while longer too.

After all, she certainly hadn't given up on getting him to help her search for her birth mother. Persistence, as her brother frequently informed her, was one of her most prominent—and irritating—characteristics.

She glanced at her travel clock sitting on the bedside

table and saw it was time to get up if she was going to shower, blow-dry her hair, dress, and drive to Potter Place by ten o'clock. She threw the blanket back and grabbed the robe she'd left lying on the foot of the bed. Chilly spring mornings were wonderful, but these old houses tended to be poorly insulated. Thank goodness the adjoining bathroom had been modernized to include an overhead heater.

An hour later, Mattie pulled up in front of Potter Place. She sat in her car a minute, looking with a writer's eye at the way sunlight filtered through the emerging leaves of the massive maples that flanked the front walk. A small redbud and half a dozen white dogwoods off to the side of the yard were just coming into bloom, and a rectangular bed filled with daffodils brightened the near corner of the lot. Tomorrow morning, she decided, she would come back earlier with her camera and get some shots while the light was still soft.

In the meantime, her stomach reminded her that it was past her usual breakfast hour. She opened her car door and stepped into the street. At that moment, Denver came around the corner of the cottage carrying a tray laden with a variety of dishes. He spotted her and grinned.

Mattie pulled in a deep breath. My, but Denver looked fabulous this morning in a pair of snug jeans that had faded to a soft blue. His bright blue golf shirt highlighted his eyes, and his dark hair, which he wore a bit shorter than Mattie would have preferred, stopped about an inch above his shoulders.

"Get a grip, girl," Mattie murmured to herself. "He may be cute but you don't have time for a crush." Taking another deep breath, she called out, "Good morning. Do you need any help?"

Denver nodded toward the front porch. "Just open the door for me, please."

"Sure thing." Mattie hurried up the steps and pulled the screen door open. The inside door was already ajar.

Denver shot her a smile of thanks as he passed, holding the tray in front of him. The unmistakable fragrances of sausage and cheese floated in his wake. Mattie's mouth watered and she quickly stepped inside to follow Denver to the kitchen.

He had already set the table using the pretty pink dishes, and he'd centered the table with a white bud vase holding one perfect daffodil. Touched that he had gone to so much trouble, Mattie hurried to clear a spot on the cabinet for him to set the tray.

"Something smells good," she said. She heaved a sigh of delight when Denver lifted the lid from a casserole dish to reveal a combination of sausage, eggs, and chopped green pepper. When he uncovered a second bowl, Mattie moaned softly. "That just has to be cheese grits."

Denver gazed at the contents of the bowl and frowned. "If you say so. Is there supposed to be butter floating on the top like that?"

Mattie laughed. "Spoken like a true Yankee. Obviously

Beth Ann has had a hand in cooking breakfast. But have you never eaten cheese grits before?"

"I've never eaten any kind of grits before, cheese or otherwise. And frankly, I don't see any reason to start now."

Mattie cocked her head to one side. "Well, come to think of it, I don't see any reason you should start now either. Can I have the leftovers?"

Denver raised his brows high, then twirled the ends of an imaginary mustache. "Ah! I see through your nefarious plan. You want to save all the cheese grits for yourself. In that case, I'll just have to eat a huge serving."

"Zounds! Foiled again," Mattie said, playing along.

Denver laughed, then picked up the breakfast casserole and carried it to the table. "There's orange juice in the fridge, already poured, and the coffee's ready. I hope I didn't make it too strong for you."

"I don't think that's possible. Besides, I have my lovely flavored cream just in case."

"That you do." Denver returned to the tray and picked up the cheese grits. "Well, darn."

"What?"

"I forgot the biscuits."

"No you didn't." Mattie's nose had told her there were biscuits wrapped in the colorful terry cloth towel that lined a flat basket. "They're right here." She pulled the towel back. "Along with some butter and jelly. Looks as though Beth Ann thought of everything."

"I've got a wonderful sister-in-law. I'm going to take that lady out to dinner sometime this week."

"Oh? Are you planning on staying a few more days then?"

Mattie watched as a slight frown touched Denver's brow. "I'm not sure yet. Maybe. Are you ready to eat?"

Obviously Denver wasn't comfortable talking about his plans, so Mattie decided to let the subject drop. For the moment, at least. "I'm more than ready to eat. Let's get the food on the table and dig in."

Denver nodded his agreement and quickly carried the cheese grits to the table. Mattie followed with the biscuits.

"I'll get the coffee," Denver offered, then poured two cups and carried them to the table. "I even put some of your cream in that little pink pitcher, but I left it in the fridge so it wouldn't spoil."

"Thanks. I'll get it and the orange juice too." By the time Mattie retrieved the cream pitcher and juice, Denver stood behind her chair, ready to seat her at the table. It had been a number of years since a man had performed that small courtesy for her, and she couldn't help being impressed. "Thanks," she murmured, taking her seat.

Half an hour later, both she and Denver leaned back in their chairs and groaned. "I can't believe I ate that much breakfast," Mattie said.

"Same here. Especially after you talked me into trying the cheese grits. They're not bad."

Mattie grinned. "Too bad you had to eat three servings before you could decide whether you liked them or not."

Denver grinned back. "I don't jump to hasty conclusions. In this case, I decided I liked them, but they sure are rich."

"True. In fact, I ate so much of everything Beth Ann sent us that I'll have to run a few miles to work it off."

"Do you enjoy running?"

"Most of time I do. But some days I just do it for my health. Do you run?"

"Yeah. Actually, my house is near a neighborhood high school and I run on the school's track. It's handy, and lots of the neighbors run there too."

"That sounds wonderful. I travel so much I have to depend on a treadmill more often than I'd like."

"You like to travel?"

"I love it, which is fortunate, because my job requires a lot of travel."

"Seems like a lot of people do enjoy traveling, at least for a while. Then it gets old."

"Are you speaking from experience?"

Denver smiled and shook his head. "Not me. The farthest I travel on my job is the nine miles from my house to the office. And that's enough for me."

"But you're here now," Mattie pointed out.

Denver shrugged. "You know, it's funny how things work out. Three years ago I'd never heard of Barbourville, Tennessee, and then Megan ended up spending a summer here, so Dayton, Dallas, and I drove down one day to check on her."

"What do you mean—check on her?"

"The three of us had promised our late sister, Megan's mom, to watch over Megan, and we took that responsibility seriously. Megan had been on her way to Chicago to visit us when she got sidetracked here in Barbourville, and we were afraid she was being intimidated by the local sheriff. It soon became obvious she was holding her own with him. She married him that fall and gave birth to their three girls the next summer."

"I've already seen the triplets. They're dolls. Hey, does that mean that triplets run in your family?"

"Apparently. There were triplets in my grandmother's family, then me and my brothers, and now Megan's girls."

"I don't think I've heard what she named them."

"Probably not. Everybody just refers to them as The Girls. Their names are Deanna, Susanna, and Brianna. We'll probably end up calling them Dee, Sue, and Bri, that is, if we ever get to the point where we can tell them apart."

Mattie laughed. "That will be a challenge until they develop their own personalities. Then it should get easier. Now that I know you and Dallas, I don't have a bit of trouble telling you apart."

Denver's brows shot up. "Really?"

"Absolutely. You're much more laid back than Dallas."

"That's pretty perceptive of you. My Mom says that's because I was always the brother in the middle. Dayton was the arrogant one and Dallas was cocky as all get-out, so they usually ended up wanting to go in two different directions at the same time. I was the brother who tried to keep them from going too far out in left field, so to speak."

Mattie nodded. "I can envision that already, although I've never met Dayton, of course. Does he visit here often?"

"As often as he can. Right now he's holding the fort down in Chicago, what with me being away. We've got some other excellent attorneys in the firm though, so he'll be fine."

"That's good," Mattie murmured. She'd been making small talk, trying to work up her courage. Now was the time, she decided. She pulled in a shallow breath and forced a smile she hoped didn't look too artificial. "If you're thinking about staying in Barbourville a few days, does that mean you've reconsidered about helping me search for my mother?"

Denver's gaze grew solemn. "I've thought about it a lot but I still don't know where we'd start. What makes you think your mother is in Barbourville anyway?"

"Fair question," Mattie said with an emphatic nod. "It's a long story, but I'll make it as brief as I can and if you have questions, then I'll try to answer them."

Denver leaned back in his chair. "Go ahead then."

"When I decided I wanted to find my birth mother, I asked my adoptive parents for information. They were understanding and perfectly willing to tell me all they knew. It seems that one of Mom's cousins knew Mom and Dad wanted to adopt, and when she heard from a friend that a baby was available through the Adoption and Love Agency in Mississippi, she notified Mom. Dad called the agency's phone number and was told that he and Mom could adopt a baby but since they were from Georgia, they'd have to pay a larger fee than most. They agreed to bring five thousand dollars with them when they drove to Mississippi to pick up the baby. They met with a man who claimed he was the agency's attorney, gave him the money, signed some papers, and were handed a baby, which was me."

"Was it all a scam?" Denver asked.

"That's pretty much what I discovered. As soon as I started investigating, I learned the Adoption and Love Agency had never existed."

"Is it possible your folks had the name wrong?"

"No. The agency name was on the papers they were given at the time of my adoption. But it was definitely a fictitious name. My adoptive parents had been duped."

"That must have come as quite a shock to them."

"To all of us actually. I hadn't expected a setback so soon. But fortunately, Mom remembered the name of the man who had claimed to represent the agency and I immediately headed to Mississippi to hunt up Arnold Lipp."

"That would be the man your Mom remembered?"

"Right. The town, Kirkland, was a fairly small one and I quickly discovered that Arnold Lipp, who had been a prominent attorney, had died five years previously. Fortunately, his wife still lived there. She didn't know anything about her husband arranging for an adoption. In fact, he had been in his last year of law school the year I was born, and she didn't even know him at that time. She'd gone to college in Mississippi, but Mr. Lipp had gone out of state to a college in Massachusetts."

Denver leaned forward. "So what did you do then?"

"I asked for the names of some of Mr. Lipp's friends, which his wife kindly supplied, and then I started looking them up and asking questions. Most of them didn't know Mr. Lipp when I was born, but I finally hooked up with one who had gone to high school and college with him. This fellow gave me the name of Mr. Lipp's college roommate but he didn't know where the roommate lives now."

"But you were able to track him down," Denver stated with some certainty.

"Actually, I ended up hiring a private investigator because I didn't have the time to devote to the task. Fortunately, the PI found Mr. Lipp's old roommate, a man named Ronald Pollitt, without too much trouble. Mr. Pollitt said he wasn't aware that Mr. Lipp had handled an adoption but he did remember Mr. Lipp taking off one year in the middle of spring semester and heading to Mississippi. All Mr. Lipp ever said about the trip was that he was doing a big favor for a buddy. He didn't name the buddy, but Mr. Pollitt noticed that another classmate, a man whose last name was McCray, was missing from classes during the same time period. The McCray man and Mr. Lipp returned to school at the same time, and the next week Mr. Lipp bought a new car."

Denver raised his brows. "That certainly sounds suspicious. But there must be a lot of McCrays in the world. Did your PI identify one of the McCrays from McCray County?"

"He discovered that there were two McCrays—Josh and Richard—both from McCray County, enrolled in that university at that time. Those two McCrays and no more."

Denver frowned. "Refresh my memory. Josh McCray is the attorney and Richard McCray is the architect, right?"

"Yes, and neither has ever married."

"So what do you suspect? Do you think one of them is your father?"

"I think it's more likely that my mother is from Barbourville and that she turned to one of the McCray brothers for help when she got pregnant. I also think that one of the McCrays, probably Josh because he was enrolled in law school, turned to Arnold Lipp for help and Mr. Lipp in turn went home to Mississippi to arrange the adoption in return for the fee my adoptive parents paid."

Denver's frown deepened. "There's a lot of supposition in your story. But if you're correct, why not go to Josh McCray and ask him if what you believe is true?"

"Because if it is, and if my mother wants to remain anonymous, he'll merely warn her and she could go further underground before I have a chance to contact her and explain that all I want from her is my medical background."

"You could ask Josh to tell her that."

"Sure, but she might not believe that's my real reason for contacting her. She might feel it was a ruse on my part. I'm not willing to take that chance if I can help it."

Denver leaned back in his chair again. "You've got a point about the possibility of her thinking it's a ruse. After all, a lot of adopted people never know who their birth parents are, and they don't seem to have a problem living without knowing."

Mattie sighed. "I can see that I'm not even convincing *you* that my sense of urgency is justified. I would have even less luck convincing Josh McCray, especially if he really is hiding something."

"You may be right about that. But you mentioned a sense of urgency. Is there something you're not telling me?"

She took a deep breath, then expelled it quickly. "Have you ever heard of Raynaud's Disease?"

Denver shook his head slowly. "No, I haven't. What is it?"

"It's a condition in which blood vessels, usually in your hands and feet, overreact to cold temperatures and slow down blood flow in order to preserve the body's core temperature. My first occurrence of the problem developed this past winter. When I'd be out in the cold for a few minutes, I'd notice a really strange feeling in a couple of fingers on each hand. When I looked at them, about half of each finger would be totally white, obviously with no blood at all reaching the tips."

"That's weird."

"It sure is. So of course I did some research and discovered that it's a condition with a name. Raynaud's Disease varies from one person to another, and so far, it's merely a nuisance for me. But for people who live in cold climates, Raynaud's Disease can present more of a danger."

"But you don't live in a cold climate, do you?"

"No, my apartment is near my parents' house in Georgia."

"I'm guessing that you feel you've inherited the condition," Denver said. "But if it's just a nuisance, what's the urgency in finding your birth parents?"

"If it's an inherited condition, there would be no real urgency," Mattie agreed. "The problem arises if it's *not* inherited."

Denver stared at her a few seconds. "Okay, I'll ask the obvious. What's the big deal if it's not inherited."

"Then I could be in real trouble. You see—" The sudden slamming of the screen door interrupted her. A second later, Dallas' voice sounded from the front of the house. "Is anybody home?"

Mattie was well aware that there was only one acceptable response to that question. "Come on back, Dallas. We're still at the breakfast table."

A few seconds later, Dallas stepped into the kitchen. His gaze quickly swept across the table and then to Mattie's and Denver's faces. "Am I interrupting something?"

"Not at all." Mattie jumped to her feet. She stood for a minute, looking first at Denver and then at Dallas. This was the first time she'd seen the brothers in the same room, and she was eager to see how much they differed in appearance.

A stranger, she decided, might have trouble telling one from the other. For her, the differences were obvious. Dallas' self-assured stance and the knowing glint in his eyes suggested he still maintained the cocky attitude Denver had described earlier. Denver's bearing, on the other hand, exuded quiet confidence and an easygoing manner. She decided she was more comfortable with Denver's personality than with his brother's. But a person couldn't help liking Dallas, of course.

"There's coffee left," she said. "Would you like a cup?"

"Yes, I would, thanks." He pulled a chair out, sat down at the table, and reached for a cold biscuit. Then, helping himself to Denver's bread plate and knife, he halved the biscuit and reached for the jam.

"Make yourself at home, why don't you?" Denver said with heavy sarcasm.

Dallas made a point of looking around the kitchen. "I thought I was at home. Last time I looked, *my* name was on the deed to this place."

Denver affected a menacing glare. "Your name may also be carved on a tombstone in the near future if you start hassling me."

Dealing with Denver

Mattie grinned as she placed a cup of coffee in front of Dallas. "Now boys, behave yourselves."

Dallas grinned back. "You sound just like Beth Ann."

"I consider that a compliment." Mattie sat down across from Denver and looked at Dallas. "I hope you didn't come to pick up the dishes. I want to wash them before I return them."

Dallas' quick frown of confusion indicated that the dishes were the furthest thing from his mind. "No, don't worry about the dishes. We've got plenty." He spread jam on his biscuit. "I just came over to tell my brother that Dayton called this morning."

"So?" Denver asked. "How are things in Chicago?"

"Fine. He just wanted to see how everybody's getting along down here. I told him you were going to stay for a few days." Dallas took another bite of biscuit.

"So?"

"So, after he picked himself up off the floor, he asked which alien spaceship had abducted our brother and left you in his place."

Mattie had been following the brothers' conversation, first with amusement, but now with confusion. "Why would Dayton ask something like that?"

Dallas glanced at Denver, who met his gaze. It was obvious to Mattie that some communication passed between the brothers. "Just an old family joke," Dallas said. "So what are you young people planning to do today?"

"We don't have any plans," Denver responded. "What are you old folks going to do?"

Dallas grinned. "Beth Ann wants to have a cookout this afternoon. The weather is supposed to be unseasonably warm, so she's invited half the town over for hamburgers and hot dogs. She specifically told me to insist that you join us, Mattie."

Mattie didn't hesitate. This would be a perfect opportunity to meet some of the people she'd hoped to become acquainted with in Barbourville. "I'd love to come. What time? And can I help Beth Ann with the preparations?"

"Around six. And I don't know about Beth Ann, but I'd welcome some help. I've been assigned the task of getting the lawn furniture cleaned up. This will be the first time we've used it this season."

Denver snorted. "You are such a slug. You'll have Trevor and me to help you. You don't need to impose on Mattie."

"No, I'd love to help," Mattie said, getting to her feet. "When are you starting?"

"Around two. Just come on over. I'll be in the side yard with buckets of sudsy water. Beth Ann informed me that we need to get all the furniture washed ahead of time so it will have time to dry before our guests get here."

Mattie glanced at the wall clock, an old-fashioned black cat with a clock in its belly and a tail that swung from side to side in time with the passing seconds. "Fine. That means I'll have time to wash up your dishes before we come over."

She stood and started stacking the dirty plates. "And Denver will help me, I'm sure."

Denver got to his feet slowly, then shot his brother a knowing glance. "Looks like us *young people* will have plenty to do this afternoon after all."

Dallas just grinned and grabbed another biscuit before he turned and hurried from the room.

Five

Denver didn't mind helping Mattie with the dishes. Living alone, he'd had plenty of experience with kitchen chores.

But he couldn't help wishing Dallas hadn't interrupted them before Mattie could tell him exactly what she considered to be so urgent about her illness. Obviously she was in no mood to talk about it after Dallas left. She'd immediately started carrying their breakfast dishes to the sink.

"Do you want to wash or dry?" Denver asked.

"I'll wash, if you don't mind. I hate drying dishes."

"Fine with me." Denver stepped over to the cabinets near the sink and pulled out the drawer where Beth Ann stored the clean dish towels.

"Do we need to fix a dish to take to the cookout?" Mattie asked.

Denver paused to think about the situation. "Well, let's see. I'm sure Daniel will bring his famous baked beans."

"The sheriff cooks?"

"From what I've heard, he's a better cook than Megan, which isn't surprising."

Mattie set a stack of dirty plates on the counter and turned to look at him. "Okay, if I'm going to be socializing with all of these people this afternoon, I need to be sure I've got everyone straight. The sheriff, Daniel McCray, is married to Megan, who is your niece, right?"

"Right."

"Why isn't it surprising that she can't cook?"

"Megan's dad is a prominent attorney in Atlanta. Her mother, my older sister, died of cancer when Megan was just a child, and her father never remarried, so Megan was mostly raised by housekeepers. She's learned to cook some dishes since she married, but she doesn't have any specialties like Daniel's baked beans or Beth Ann's burgers."

"Beth Ann's specialty is hamburgers?"

"Right. There seems to be some incident involving hamburgers in her and Dallas' past, but they just smile and clam up if anyone asks them about it."

Mattie shrugged. "Every couple has a right to a few secrets from the rest of the world." She reached under the sink for the dishwashing liquid and squirted some in the sink, then turned the water on. "Tell me what you know about the rest of the McCrays."

Denver watched her immerse their juice glasses and coffee cups in the sudsy water. "I really don't know much about them, probably not as much as you already know. I can tell you that the judge, Daniel's uncle Bob, is a character. He likes to interfere in other people's lives, so be careful around him. I've met Daniel's other two uncles, Josh and Richard, but I haven't been around them much. On short acquaintance, I'd say they're a little reserved, and so is Daniel's father."

"His father is the mayor of Barbourville, right?"

Daniel reached into the rinse water for a coffee cup and started drying it. "Yep. His name is Bill. You'll like him, I think."

Mattie picked up Beth Ann's casserole dish and lowered it into the dishwater. "Anything else I should know about the people I'll be meeting?"

"Not that I can think of. Beth Ann doesn't have any relatives around here, but everybody in town is crazy about her."

"Yeah, I've gotten that impression. I appreciate her including me in the cookout this afternoon. But I'm really not going to feel right unless I take something."

Denver stifled a sigh. He could gauge from Mattie's tone that this was a bone she wasn't going to relinquish easily. "We could go to the store and buy some chips," he suggested.

He wasn't surprised to see Mattie shake her head. "No, that's something they'll have plenty of. I know! If you'll go to the store while I finish these dishes, I'll make a buttermilk pie."

For a second Denver thought he'd heard wrong. Then he was afraid he hadn't. "Did you say buttermilk pie?"

"Have you never eaten buttermilk pie?" Mattie obviously didn't see anything incongruous in using those two words in the same sentence, but Denver sure did.

"Nope. It doesn't seem to me that.... Well, eh, I mean, eh.... Buttermilk?" He stumbled to a halt.

Mattie grinned. "Relax. I don't like buttermilk either, but a buttermilk pie is delicious. Kind of like a chess pie, only better. Will you go to the store for me?"

"Sure." Denver didn't know where he'd find a grocery store open on Sunday, but he figured Dallas could tell him.

"Great. I know the recipe by heart. I'll just make a list for you." Mattie dried her hands and picked up the small pad lying next to the kitchen phone. "I sure do appreciate this."

"No problem." Denver had no intention of telling Mattie that while he'd be glad to buy the ingredients, nothing on earth could convince him to actually eat something called buttermilk pie.

By four o'clock that afternoon, Denver had driven twenty miles one way to find an open supermarket, helped wash lawn furniture, and assisted Mattie in making three buttermilk pies. By the time the pies were in the oven, he had discovered that Mattie possessed a wry sense of humor, and he had spent as much time laughing as he had mixing the batter for her.

He had also allowed Mattie to cajole him into promising to try a piece of the pie.

As soon as the pies were out of the oven and sitting on racks to cool, Mattie announced that she had to return to the B and B to shower and change clothes. Denver could understand her feeling. He had gotten wet and dirty while helping wash the lawn furniture because on more than one occasion, Dallas had "accidentally" turned the water hose on him and Trevor. Only when Trevor tackled Dallas and took him down on the soft spring grass did Dallas laughingly agree to behave himself.

Denver walked Mattie to her car and then returned to the cottage to shower and change clothes. He was thankful he'd packed some casual clothes for his trip to Atlanta. As it turned out, he hadn't needed them for the conference, but they were going to come in handy now.

An hour later, he settled down in the swing on the front porch to wait for Mattie. He couldn't believe how good he felt. Never had he been so content to be away from home. As a rule, Denver didn't enjoy traveling, whereas both Dayton and Dallas appeared to feel as comfortable on the road as they were between their own four walls.

Denver wasn't sure why he was so different from his brothers, but he suspected it went back to their childhoods when he'd been caught smack dab in the middle between Dayton's arrogant insistence that his way was the only way and Dallas' incessant desire to do the opposite of whatever Dayton happened to want. Having spent his youth acting as the constant between two opposing forces had left Denver craving peace and tranquility.

Maybe he really had "fallen into a rut" as everyone in his family liked to inform him. But he was happy in his rut and didn't see any sense in changing merely for the sake of change.

Which didn't explain why all of a sudden he was perfectly content to be away from his home and his routine, why this small cottage in a rural town felt as much like home to him as his much larger and more familiar house in Chicago.

He gave a mental shrug and stared down the street, watching for Mattie's car. He'd already decided to stick close by her side during the cookout. He knew perfectly well that she would be people-watching, looking for signs that might suggest she was related to someone in the crowd. If she spotted a person who felt familiar to her, he wanted to be on hand in case she needed a shoulder or a sounding board.

Five minutes later, when Mattie pulled her car up to the curb and got out, Denver went to meet her. When she stepped around the front of her car and came into full view, he stopped in his tracks. She'd changed from her jeans into a pair of long white slacks that flared a bit at the bottom and really emphasized the length of her legs. The bright pink, lacy-looking shirt she wore had a scooped neck and short sleeves and hugged her slender torso. She'd changed her running shoes for sandals, painted her toenails to match her blouse, and left her blond hair hanging loose around her shoulders. Denver pulled a deep breath into his lungs and exhaled slowly.

Apparently unaware of the effect she was having on him, Mattie smiled and stepped onto the sidewalk. "Wow, you look spiffy," she said. "That's a great shirt."

Denver glanced down at the two-tone polo his Mom had given him for his birthday last year. He couldn't remember whether he'd worn it before or not. "Thanks!"

"Is it silk?" Mattie asked. She'd stopped beside him and reached to finger the sleeve. "Feels like it."

"Hmm, I'm not sure," Denver managed to say. In addition to looking fantastic, Mattie now smelled wonderful too. "Nice perfume."

She smiled. "Thank you. If the pies have cooled enough, I want to slice them before we go."

Denver swallowed. "The pies? Oh yeah! I think they've cooled okay. By the way, you look really good yourself this afternoon."

Mattie heaved a quick sigh. "Thanks for saying that. I've been worried that I wasn't dressed right. But you do think I look okay?"

Denver decided not to tell her exactly how fantastic he thought she looked. He didn't want her to think he was trying to flatter her. So he nodded solemnly. "You look just perfect to me. Now, let's go check on those pies."

He motioned her to lead the way up the sidewalk and across the porch, and then he stepped forward to pull the screen door open for her. He knew Mattie would be looking for a resemblance between herself and everyone else at the cookout, but he was very much afraid that she was going to be disappointed.

Because there was no one in Barbourville, he was convinced, who would be even half as beautiful as Mattie this afternoon.

* * *

Ten minutes later, after she'd cut each of the pies into eighths, Mattie loaded two onto a tray for Denver to carry. She picked up the third, moistened her lips, and pulled in a deep breath. Darn but she wished her stomach would settle down. Unfortunately, a bad case of nerves usually set her stomach to spinning.

And she was certainly nervous about this cookout. What if she should see someone she felt certain was her mother? Or even her father? What if one of them was there and recognized her?

Denver picked up the tray that held the pies. "Are you ready?" he asked.

Merciful heavens no, she wasn't ready, but she could hardly say so. She forced a smile. "Absolutely. I can smell those hamburgers cooking already."

Which was true. Earlier Denver had opened the kitchen windows to let some fresh air in, and now it was accompanied by the alluring odor of charcoal and Beth Ann's hamburgers. The sound of laughter floated inside along with the scented air. Obviously the guests had started arriving.

"Okay," Denver said, returning her smile. "Let's go then. And Mattie?"

She paused and looked at him. His smile had faded and a slight frown pulled at his brows. "If you see anyone you think looks familiar, let me know. I'll see what I can find out about the person for you, but you need to be careful not to give anything away about your suspicions in case that person has something to hide from you."

Mattie's stomach immediately settled down, and the smile she sent his way was sincere rather than forced. "Thanks, Denver. I really appreciate this."

He smiled back. "You're welcome. Ready?"

"Let's go."

Mattie led the way, holding a pie in one hand and opening doors for Denver, who had both hands tied up carrying the tray. They'd barely stepped onto the porch when Trevor came running up.

"Mom said you might need some help," he said, reaching for Mattie's pie. "Wow! This smells good. What is it?"

"Pie," Denver said.

Trevor sniggered. "I know that, Uncle Denver. What kind?"

"Best you just think of it as pie, son."

"Oh, for heaven's sake," Mattie said, pretending to be offended. "It's buttermilk pie, and it's ever bit as good as it smells."

Trevor widened his eyes. "Okay, Miss Meadows. I'll

take your word for it and have a piece of it later. Guess what else we have for dessert?"

"What?" Denver wanted to know.

"Miss Jill—the lady who owns that new restaurant in town—she brought one of her specialties, a Hummingbird Cake.

"Great," Mattie said.

"That's strange," Denver added.

"What? The name of the cake?"

"No, I've had Hummingbird Cake before, in Atlanta. A friend of Megan's—her name was Jill too—always had a Hummingbird Cake made to share with us when we visited Megan and her dad."

"That's the same lady," Trevor said. "She moved here a while back and opened a restaurant."

They rounded the end of the hedge that separated the cottage's back yard from Dallas' and Beth Ann's back yard. "Oh, wow!" Trevor said. "Look at that crowd. This is the first cookout of the season and I think everybody's going to show up." He turned to address Mattie. "I just saw one of my friends arrive. Is it okay if I put this pie with the desserts and go see him?"

"Certainly," Mattie said. "You run along."

"Thanks." Trevor jogged to the picnic table that had obviously been designated to hold desserts, deposited the pie, and took off in a hard run toward one of the cars that now lined Redbud Road.

"He's a nice kid," Mattie noted.

"You're right about that." Denver glanced around. "I see Dallas manning the grill. Let me set these pies down and we'll go over and say hello."

The dessert table was already loaded. Mattie spotted the Hummingbird Cake, three gorgeous layers that she knew contained bananas and crushed pineapple in the batter. The cream cheese frosting had been decorated with ground pecans. "Hmmm, that looks good," she said. Denver still held the tray, so she unloaded the remaining two pies, sitting them near a beautiful banana pudding. "Oh, wow! I can tell I'm going to have to run a few miles tomorrow."

"You and me both." Denver slid the empty tray under the table. "Let's see if Dallas needs any help."

When they turned away from the table, he placed his hand on the back of her waist. Warmth, comforting and at the same time strangely exhilarating, spread up her back. She leaned back a fraction, and the pressure of his hand increased, as though silently projecting a promise of constancy and support.

Mattie's eyes widened. Her reaction to Denver's closeness amazed her. She couldn't recall ever having felt this sense of safety and of support that seemed to be a common occurrence whenever she was with him.

But there was no time for further contemplation. They weren't halfway across the lawn yet and already half a dozen people had started toward them. Mattie recognized the sheriff of course. Daniel McCray wasn't a man anyone would be likely to forget. Tall and handsome, with gorgeous topaz eyes, he was conscientious and understanding and madly in love with his wife. Megan walked beside him, her hand clasped in his, but their triplets were nowhere to be seen.

After ensuring that Mattie had already met Daniel and Megan, Denver looked at Megan and demanded, "What have you done with my great nieces?"

Megan laughed. She was a pretty woman with chestnut hair and a trim figure. "Beth Ann took them into the house. She said she was afraid there might be mosquitoes out tonight, but Dallas says it's too early for mosquitoes and that Beth Ann was just looking for an excuse to make off with the girls."

"Probably just as well," Denver said, gazing around at the growing crowd. "They'd be passed around like dolls if they were outside. Here come a couple of your uncles, Daniel. Why don't you introduce them to Mattie."

"Glad to," Daniel said. He waved to the two men who had stopped nearby, apparently waiting to join the group but not wanting to interrupt. "Uncle Josh, Uncle Richard, come here. I want you to meet the young lady who's writing an article about Potter Place."

Mattie held her breath as Josh and Richard approached. Here were the two McCray brothers who had been in college in Massachusetts while the man who had arranged for her adoption was enrolled there. Daniel introduced Josh first, followed by Richard. When each smiled and shook her hand, Mattie took the opportunity to study them. Both were older versions of Daniel McCray, possessing the same pleasant features, blue-green eyes, and charming smiles. If she resembled either in any way, she couldn't see it.

She glanced at Denver, who obviously had been following her line of thought. He looked into her eyes and gave a very tiny shake of his head. Apparently he didn't see any resemblance either.

Then Daniel's third uncle, the judge, hurried up to the group. He was the oldest of the McCray brothers and also the most charming. Mattie had met him her first day in town when he'd made a point to stop by the cottage to check her out.

"Why, Miz Meadows." He reached to grasp her hand. "I'm sure happy to see that you're still gracing our little town with your presence. You haven't finished that article yet, I assume."

Mattie suppressed a chuckle. The judge was a delight as long as you understood that he was an intellectual masquerading as a good old boy. "I want to do the cottage justice, Judge McCray. That's a concept you understand, I'm sure."

"Justice?" He threw his head back and laughed. "I certainly hope so. I like you, Miz Meadows. You're a lady after my own heart."

Before Mattie had a chance to respond, another man joined the group. He stopped beside the judge and grinned. "Okay, Bob, what are you up to now?"

This man had to be Bill, the fourth brother, Mattie realized, taking in his topaz eyes and handsome features. Slightly younger than the judge, Bill was the mayor of Barbourville and father to the sheriff.

Daniel made the introductions, and the mayor pronounced himself delighted to make Mattie's acquaintance. "We're very pleased that you're writing about Potter Place," he told her. Then he turned to Denver. "Just as we're pleased to have Dallas renovating all of this property around here. The tax base is growing pretty rapidly."

"I'm glad to hear it," Denver said.

Just as he spoke, another guest joined their group. A pretty but petite lady with soft brown hair and large brown eyes stepped up close to Josh McCray's side. A gentle smile touched his lips, and he wrapped an arm around her shoulders.

"Hello, my dear," he said. "I'm so glad you could come. I want to introduce you to Mattie Meadows, the young woman who's writing an article about the cottage. And Mattie, this is Lily Martin, the town librarian and a very dear friend of mine."

Mattie took a deep breath, forced a bright smile, and reached to grasp the hand the woman had held out to her. At this moment, she realized, although there was no way for her to know for sure, there was at least a possibility that she was shaking hands with her mother.

The woman's grasp was firm and her smile was welcoming. "I'm so pleased to meet you, Miss Meadows. The town has been abuzz about a travel writer being in our midst. How long do you plan to be with us?"

"I'm not entirely sure yet," Mattie said, staring hard at the woman, seeking a hint of familiarity, but the arrival of two more women claimed her attention.

The first to join their circle was tall and strikingly handsome, with dark hair pulled back in a severe bun. She wore black slacks with a soft gray blouse and black loafers. She watched Mattie, even as she stepped to Richard McCray's side.

A slight movement from Richard caught Mattie's attention and her gaze dropped to his hand. He had started to reach for the newcomer's elbow, then stopped himself and thrust his hand into the pocket of his slacks instead.

The woman didn't wait for introductions. "Good evening, everyone." Her gaze swept all of the faces in the circle, then paused on Mattie's. She held her hand out to Mattie. "Hello. I'm Eloise Smithfield, Richard's business partner. You must be Mattie Meadows."

Mattie reached to shake hands. "Yes. It's nice to meet you."

The second newcomer had appeared to hold back for a minute but she now stepped forward to join the circle. Mattie instantly envisioned this lady as the perfect model for Mrs. Santa Claus with her beautiful white hair and pleasantly rotund figure. She wore a split skirt and knit shirt and a slightly shy smile. She opened her mouth but before she managed to get any words out, the judge stepped to her side and wrapped an arm around her.

"And here's my dear wife," he said. "Miz Meadows, I want to introduce you to Miz Evelyn, the love of my life and the best cook in the state of Tennessee, bar none."

A blush brightened the woman's cheeks. "Now, Bob, don't make claims I can't live up to. As a matter of fact, I saw three of the most beautiful buttermilk pies on the dessert table, and I suspect our guest brought those. Would I be right, Miss Meadows?"

Mattie grinned. "If I'm being judged by the best cook in the state, I may plead the fifth."

Evelyn McCray laughed. "No need to do that. I confess I sneaked a small piece, and it's fantastic. I'd almost forgotten buttermilk pie, and I don't know why. It was my grandmother's specialty."

The judge smiled and gazed at his wife with pride plainly written on his face. "We'll have to invite Miz Meadows to dinner one evening soon, my dear." He turned to Mattie. "There's nothing Miz Evelyn and I enjoy more than having folks over to dinner."

Mattie nodded. "I'd be delighted." She paused and scanned the group. "But, please, everyone, call me Mattie."

Almost everyone in the group smiled and nodded, then looked around as Dallas gave a shout to say that the burgers were ready and dinner was being served. The older people hung back and allowed the younger members of the group to get in line first.

A polite clamor ensued and Mattie took the opportunity to look around her. She wasn't at all sure she would recognize either her mother or her father even if one or both were present.

In a way, she was just as glad. While it was true that she needed to know who her parents were, for tonight she wanted to relax and enjoy the company of some very nice people.

And most of all, she realized, she wanted to spend as much time as possible this evening with Denver. She understood that soon they'd go their separate ways so she questioned her wisdom in deepening their friendship, but that didn't change her desire to get to know him better.

Six

The cookout proved to be so popular that it was dark before people started gathering up their dishes, thanking Beth Ann and Dallas, and calling cheerful good-byes to each other.

Denver had kept watch over Mattie, concerned that she might feel uncomfortable mingling with a group of strangers when there was a possibility that one or both of her birth parents were among those present. Perhaps it was his imagination, but he was almost positive that anytime he and Mattie drifted apart, she soon looked around for him and whenever she saw him nearby, her shoulders visibly relaxed.

Now, with the party winding down, he stepped to her side. "Ready to call it an evening?"

"Sure am. Just give me a second to thank Beth Ann and Dallas. Then I'll help you carry the pie pans back to the cottage."

Denver didn't really need help carrying three empty pie pans, but he quickly accepted Mattie's offer. "Thanks. How about a cup of decaf before you go back to the B and B? I have a pot ready to brew."

"That sounds wonderful." Mattie grinned. "You're a man after my own heart. Most people complain when I want to end the day with a cup of coffee."

"Yeah, but those same people think nothing of ending their day with a soft drink full of caffeine."

Mattie laughed. "You have a point. Just give me a minute and we'll go brew that coffee."

Denver watched Mattie thread her way through the dwindling crowd so she could speak to Beth Ann and Dallas. A couple of minutes later, she rejoined him and they strolled back to the cottage.

Soon they were seated at the round kitchen table cradling cups of coffee in their hands. Mattie had cooled hers with some of her flavored cream, so she took a sip first.

"So what did you think?" Denver asked.

She placed her cup back in her saucer. "I didn't see a soul who looked familiar in any way. Of course, I didn't really expect to immediately spot someone I felt certain was my parent, either mother or father."

"Yeah, that wasn't likely to happen." Dallas lifted his cup and checked the temperature of his coffee, then set it back down. "Have you given any thought to what you'd like to try next?"

"Well, I have thought about checking with the county

newspaper to see if their files go back to the period around my birth date. These little weekly newspapers used to have lots of local gossip."

"What kind of gossip?"

"Oh, simple things, such as 'Mary Smith was out of town last week visiting her sister in Kalamazoo,' that type of thing. I might luck into a note about an absent citizen that would give me a clue."

Denver frowned. "That's a long shot."

"Maybe. Maybe not. It depends on whether the McCray brothers in some way really did have something to do with the man who arranged my adoption. I would imagine that the McCrays were considered especially newsworthy in those days."

"You may have a point. Could I come along when you visit the newspaper?"

"Sure. I could use some help looking through the back files."

Denver wrinkled his brow in thought. "I'll be glad to try, but I'm not sure I'd pick up on the type of tidbit you're looking for."

"That's okay. I usually include some of a town's history in my articles. You could watch for page-one type stories about special events in Barbourville's past."

Denver nodded. "I could do that. But if you really want to bring the town itself into the article, you'll need to do even more research."

Mattie took a sip of coffee. "True. Any suggestions?"

"You could participate in some of the town's traditions, such as eating at Sonny's Diner."

"Okay. That's in the downtown area, right?"

"Right. According to what Dallas has told me, everybody who *is* anybody goes to the Diner. How about we meet there for breakfast tomorrow morning?"

"Fine with me. And after that we'll check out the newspaper office."

"Right. And back to Sonny's for lunch."

Mattie's brows shot up. "Sonny's for both breakfast and lunch? That seems a little extreme. Why don't we have lunch at Jill's Soup Bowl? She can probably use our business. When I was visiting with her earlier this evening, several people stopped by to compliment her on the Hummingbird Cake, and most of them said they'd be trying out her restaurant since they liked that cake so much. I got the distinct impression that very few people have been patronizing her place."

Denver grimaced. "You go ahead, but I'll pass. I don't think Jill would be too thrilled about having me as a customer. She certainly went out of her way to avoid me tonight."

"I didn't notice that. Why on earth would she want to avoid you?"

"She was probably afraid I'd ask her why she left a flourishing practice in Atlanta to move to Barbourville and open a restaurant that apparently isn't doing especially well."

"What kind of practice did she have in Atlanta?"

"She trained as a psychologist and had her own counseling business the last I knew of her. She and Megan were best friends all through high school and college, so I'm assuming that's how she learned about Barbourville. But I can't begin to guess why she would want to leave Atlanta."

"And I still don't understand why she would want to avoid you."

"I'm not sure myself, but I suspect it has something to do with Dayton."

"Your brother?"

"Right. Jill's had a crush on Dayton since she was a teenager. Everybody knew that except Dayton. He just thought of her as Megan's friend and nothing more. I suspect she doesn't want him to know she's here and she's afraid I'll tell him."

"And will you?"

"Nope." Denver shrugged. "None of my business. But I don't want to make Jill uncomfortable, so I won't join you at her restaurant."

Mattie nodded. "That's nice of you. And I agree that you should probably avoid her place if it's going to make her uncomfortable. I'll try to stop by there myself when I get a chance, just to throw some business her way. In the meantime, I'd better go back to the B and B so I can get a few hours of sleep before morning. What time should we go to breakfast?"

"We'd better get to Sonny's no later than eight o'clock. I have the impression that a lot of people stop by the Diner on their way to work and if so, that would be a good opportunity for us to meet some folks."

"Okay. Do you want me to join you at the Diner or should we get together here at the cottage?"

"Why don't you come by here? You can park your car out front and we'll walk to the Diner. We might run into more people that way."

"Sounds good." Mattie pushed her coffee cup back and stood. "I'd better be on my way."

Denver also stood. "I'll follow you back to the B and B again."

Mattie opened her mouth as though to protest, then closed it again. "All right."

Fifteen minutes later, Denver stopped his car beside Mattie's in the parking lot of the bed and breakfast. As he had done the previous night, he quickly exited his car and hurried to open Mattie's door for her.

And, just as had happened the night before, when he held his hand out to her and she placed her hand in his, sensations he'd never before experienced inundated him. He felt a smile pulling at the corners of his lips. Mattie's mere touch brought with it happiness, contentment, and, at the same time, a hunger for more than just holding hands.

Denver decided on the spot that tonight when he walked Mattie to the door, he was going to kiss her. At least he would if she'd allow it.

As they walked hand in hand down the path toward the entrance to the bed and breakfast, perspiration began to coat Denver's palm. Blast it! He hadn't felt this way around a girl since his first date in high school.

Get a grip, he told himself. He didn't want Mattie thinking he was an immature schoolboy. He wanted her to think of him as—

Gravel crunched as another car pulled into the parking lot. Headlights momentarily brightened the path to the B and B entrance, and Mattie gently extracted her hand from his grasp. A second later, a car door slammed, immediately followed by the sound of footsteps behind them.

Mattie glanced over her shoulder, then stopped and turned to address the person now walking toward them. "Hello, Mrs. Dunmore. You're out late tonight."

The co-owner of the bed and breakfast hurried to join them. "Good evening, Miss Meadows. I understand you've decided to stay with us a few more days."

Mattie returned her smile. "Yes, I was delighted this morning when your husband said my room would be available for however long I want to stay. That's very accommodating of you."

"Not at all, my dear." The white-haired innkeeper looked at Denver. "You must be Dallas Vance's brother."

"I am, yes." Denver suppressed a sigh as he realized that his chances for a moment alone with Mattie had just disappeared. "And you would be Mrs. Dunmore obviously."

The woman stuck out her hand. "Are you Denver or Dayton?"

"Sorry, I should have said. I'm Denver." He shook hands with the woman, whose grip was pleasantly firm.

"No apologies necessary, Mr. Vance. You should join us for breakfast in the morning. As Miss Meadows can tell you, I serve a nice variety."

Mattie spoke up. "I'd intended to tell you, Mrs. Dunmore, that I won't be here for breakfast in the morning. Denver and I have plans. I'm sorry."

"Oh, that's perfectly all right, my dear. And I appreciate your letting me know. There aren't any other guests staying with us this early in the year, so I won't bother with anything special tomorrow morning."

She glanced at Denver, then turned back to Mattie. "But some other morning while you're here, you should invite your young man to have breakfast with us. Just give me a day's notice, and I'll fix something extra special."

"That sounds wonderful," Mattie responded. She turned to Denver. "Good night, then. I'll see you in the morning."

There was nothing Denver could do but say good night and walk back to his car while Mattie accompanied Mrs. Dunmore into the B and B. But still there was a certain spring in his step that wasn't usually there. He might have missed out on his kiss, but for some reason, the realization that Mattie had seemed to accept his designation as "her young man" brought a silly smile to his face.

It wasn't until two hours later while he was lying in bed futilely trying to sleep that he recalled his and Mattie's interrupted conversation from this morning. He never had asked her why it was so important that her Raynaud's Disease turn out to be an inherited condition.

* * *

At twenty minutes until eight the following morning, Mattie tapped on the front door of Potter Place. The morning air was cool but the sun was bright, suggesting that the day would warm up considerably as the hours passed. When she dressed that morning, she had decided on her navy cotton slacks topped by a short-sleeved tan knit shirt and a lightweight navy jacket.

While waiting for Denver to answer the door, she set her large handbag on the porch floor and pulled deep breaths into her lungs. When writing about rental accommodations, she liked to describe the fragrances guests might expect when they stayed there. Once she'd visited an inn in the country where the predominant early-morning odor came from the adjoining barnyard. This morning, fortunately, all she smelled was clean air and the faint musty fragrance of damp earth.

A couple of minutes later, Mattie started to wonder if perhaps Denver hadn't heard her knock. She had just raised her hand to tap on the door again when it opened. Denver, his hair still damp from the shower, wore khaki slacks with a blue and beige striped shirt and a rueful grin.

"Sorry. I overslept this morning. Come in for a second. I'll be ready soon."

"No problem. I'm early." Mattie had no intention of explaining that she'd awakened earlier than usual with a sense of anticipation that wouldn't allow her to go back to sleep. She was honest enough with herself not to pretend that her feelings resulted only from the possibility that she might turn up some information about her birth mother. More than anything, she suspected, was the enjoyment she anticipated in spending the day with Denver.

She picked up her bag and stepped inside. "I'll wait in the living room," she said.

"Thanks. I won't be long." Denver shot her an apologetic smile and disappeared up the stairs.

Mattie sat on one of the beautiful wooden chairs in the living room. Dallas had explained to her that much of the furniture in Potter Place had been handmade by the original resident of the house. Mr. Potter and his wife had been housekeeper and caretaker for the original owner of the huge Victorian house where Dallas and Beth Ann lived. Beth Ann had inherited the house from her great aunt Brenda but Dallas had completely renovated it after he and Beth Ann married.

Denver stepped back into the room. The subdued fragrance of his aftershave, which was laced with a faint hint of citrus, drifted ahead of him. "I'm ready," he said, shoving his arms into the sleeves of a tan windbreaker.

Mattie stood and almost immediately had to lock her knees. Wow! She hadn't expected the sight of Denver to leave her weak, but she hadn't expected him to look quite so handsome this morning either. She found his slightly chagrined expression quite appealing. She tore her gaze away from his face and reached for her bag. She picked it up and slung it onto her shoulder. "I'm ready too."

She'd expected Denver to turn toward the front door. Instead he walked with calm purpose to face her. He reached slowly for her bag, giving her time to object. When she didn't, he slipped his hand under the strap, eased the bag from her shoulder, and placed it on the floor. Finally, he grasped her shoulders firmly.

"I'd intended to do this last night," he said, his eyes darkening as he held her gaze. "But then Mrs. Dunmore interrupted me."

He slowly slid his hands from her shoulders and around her back until he could pull her closer. At no time did Mattie feel as though he was rushing her. In fact, she knew that if she resisted with even the flicker of a muscle, he'd step back and let her go.

But she had no desire to move away from his embrace. Instead she slipped her arms around his waist and turned her face up to welcome his kiss.

And what a kiss it was. Starting with almost unbelievable tenderness, Denver slowly increased the intensity until Mattie felt the strength seeping from the muscles in her legs and she tightened her grip around Denver's waist.

He responded by pulling her closer, then lifted one hand to cradle the back of her head. Wanting even more, Mattie angled her head and increased her response. A soft moan slipped from her throat into her mouth and through her sensitized lips, and awareness that she was feeling too much too soon caused her to pull away.

Denver released her slowly, drawing back to look deep into her eyes as though seeking an answer as to how she might be feeling.

She smiled and reached with her right hand to caress his cheek, which was soft and smooth from his recent shave. "What a lovely way to say good morning."

The question in his eyes was instantly replaced with a twinkle. "I'll second that."

Mattie sighed. "But we'd better leave if we're going to get to the Diner while the crowd is still there."

Denver sighed also. "You're right." He bent to pick up her bag and then helped her slip it back on her shoulder. A quick frown touched his forehead. "Don't you want me to carry that for you? It's darn heavy."

"I'm used to it. I always carry writing pads and plenty of pens and a small recorder in case I need to make oral notes to myself. Just the usual accoutrements of a writer."

Denver raised his eyebrows. "Okay. But if you need any help, let me know."

Mattie nodded her agreement and smiled to herself. She sure wasn't going to tell him that his kiss had left her with such a feeling of euphoria, she felt as though she could float across the floor, even with the weight of her heavy bag on her shoulder.

Seven

Mattie had to agree with Denver's assessment of the Diner as a good place to meet people. By the time they arrived, the quaint little restaurant was filled to overflowing. Chattering groups of people crowded around the rectangular tables or had squeezed into one of the booths. The smell of frying sausage vied for supremacy with the sharp fragrance of brewing coffee. Mattie was instantly enthralled with the atmosphere.

When they first walked in, Dallas, who was seated at one of the tables with the town's mayor and the county judge, waved them over. As soon as they were seated, a waitress hurried to greet them, two mugs in her hand. "Coffee?" she asked.

At their nods, she filled their cups, took their orders, and dashed away.

The judge shot Mattie one of his charming smiles. "As I told you last night, Miz Meadows, I'm glad to see you're still in town. But I would have thought you'd be in a big hurry to get your article written and turned in."

Mattie forced a smile. The judge was entirely too sharp for her comfort. "My editor is in no hurry, Judge McCray, and I want to include some background about the town itself. Where would you suggest I go in order to do some research on the history of Barbourville?"

The judge lowered his brows for a few seconds as though giving deep thought to her question. Finally he turned to his brother. "What do you think, Bill? Would Miz Lily at the library be her best bet?"

Bill McCray nodded slowly. "I suspect so. The library should have a copy of that history Miss Marshall wrote a few years back, the one she had printed over in Knoxville."

The judge sighed. "True, but you know that my dear Evelyn says that Miz Marshall got some of the facts wrong." He turned to Mattie. "My wife knows as much county history as anybody in these parts. Unfortunately, she was feeling poorly this morning and decided to stay in bed. Maybe if she's better in a day or two, you could come to the house and talk to her."

"That sounds wonderful, Judge." Mattie gave him her most dazzling smile, then dropped her gaze while she opened a couple of small containers of cream and stirred them into her coffee. She would welcome the opportunity to get better acquainted with the librarian, who was not only a good friend of Josh McCray's but also in the right age bracket to be her mother.

Dallas looked across the table at his brother. "And what are your plans for today, Denver?"

"I'm going to help Mattie."

"Oh!" Dallas' eyes widened momentarily. "I thought you might have changed your mind and be headed back to Chicago."

"Nope. Like I said yesterday, I'm going to stay in Barbourville for a few more days."

Dallas shrugged. "In that case, Beth Ann said that I should invite you and Mattie to dinner tonight."

"What time?" Denver asked.

"Around seven."

Denver looked at Mattie. "Is that okay with you?"

"That sounds wonderful." Mattie sincerely liked Beth Ann and Dallas and welcomed the opportunity to spend more time with them.

Forty-five minutes later, Mattie and Denver left the Diner and headed to the library. Mattie was looking forward to seeing Lily Martin again and was disappointed to discover she had gone to Knoxville to attend a workshop on how rural libraries could benefit from the extensive public database of historical documents posted on the Web.

The assistant librarian appeared eager to help, but when she reported that the library's only copy of Miss Marshall's history of McCray County was checked out, Mattie decided the newspaper office might have been a better place to start after all.

Dealing with Denver

After making plans to return the following day when Lily was scheduled to be back, Mattie and Denver exited the library and walked toward the downtown area. The sun shone brightly and the morning was warming up so quickly that Mattie paused on the sidewalk long enough to slip her jacket off and tie it around her waist.

Denver watched her with a slight frown. "If you're getting too warm, I'll be glad to get the car and drive us to the newspaper office."

"Thanks, but I'm fine. I think we only have a couple of blocks to go anyway. Say, is that your brother headed toward us?"

The man Mattie had spied was still a couple of blocks away, but he certainly resembled Dallas and he appeared to be in a hurry. Mattie squinted her eyes against the bright sun, hoping to see the man better. Within a few seconds, it was obvious that it was, in fact, Dallas walking toward them. Soon he was close enough to raise one arm in a gesture that indicated he wanted to see them.

"That's strange," Denver murmured. "He said he was going to a job site this morning."

Denver stepped up his pace a bit and Mattie hurried to keep up. For a minute she feared that something might be wrong with Beth Ann or one of the children but she quickly realized that Dallas' expression appeared harried rather than distressed.

Denver greeted his brother with a question. "What's up, Dallas?"

Dallas paused to catch his breath before responding with a question of his own. "Are you busy right now?"

Denver glanced at Mattie as though he didn't intend to desert their goal, but she immediately answered for him. "As a matter of fact, we just struck out at the library and will have to wait until tomorrow to catch Miss Martin. I think I'll check out the newspaper office and then I might wander around town for a little while, soaking up some atmosphere."

Denver thanked her with a warm smile, then turned to Dallas. "What do you need?"

"A couple drove up from Atlanta this morning to look at the house I'm renovating. They're interested in buying but insist that I install a security system. I tried to tell them they don't need a security system in McCray County, but they've been city people too long to feel comfortable without one. Could you come look at the place and give us some ideas on what type of security could be installed and how much it might cost?"

"I'll be glad to. I've worked with Steve enough to know my way around the security business fairly well. Do you need to go right now?"

Dallas nodded. "Yep. The Lamberts are waiting for us, and I know they want to head back to Atlanta before it gets too late. So we'll go now if Mattie doesn't mind."

"Of course I don't mind. You two go ahead. I'll do some research and then probably go back to the B and B to work on my article for a while this afternoon. After that I'll come back to your house for dinner if the invitation still stands."

Dallas grinned. "It stands, believe me. Beth Ann was baking pies when I left home this morning. One chocolate and one butterscotch. You don't want to miss out on that."

Mattie answered his grin with one of her own. "Don't worry. I wouldn't miss butterscotch pie for any amount of money."

Denver looked into her eyes. "You're sure you don't mind going on by yourself?"

"Positive. Now go. I'll see you tonight."

Denver nodded once. "Tonight," he said, then turned and walked away with Dallas. Mattie watched until they rounded a corner. Then she shrugged to herself and headed toward the newspaper office.

Barbourville's newspaper, which was published weekly, had barely begun to enter the electronic age. The editor, Jeffry Johnson III, son and grandson of former editors, had gone away to college for a degree in journalism, so he had the know-how but not the finances he needed to enter the modern world of printing.

He explained all of this to Mattie by way of apologizing for the fact that he hadn't yet scanned past issues of the paper and put the files on CDs. Thus, she would have to physically go through old cabinets in which previous editions had been filed, either neatly or haphazardly, depending on the capabilities of the file clerk during the years she wanted to research.

Mattie had expected nothing more from a small-town newspaper, so she wasn't at all dismayed to be led to a back room in the concrete block building, pointed to a row of metal file cabinets, and then left to hunt through them on her own.

After half an hour of searching, she located the newspapers for the year before she was born. Fortunately for her research, the current editor's grandmother, Mrs. Jeffry Johnson, Sr., had been society editor at that time, and she had taken her job seriously. In her weekly column, she frequently mentioned the comings and goings of the "McCray boys," Josh and Richard, who were in college in the north. Almost as often, Miss Eloise Springfield's name appeared as having traveled to and fro with Josh and Richard McCray. In her society column, Mrs. Johnson gushed with joy when all three returned "to the welcoming arms of family and friends in Barbourville" for Christmas or other breaks in the academic year.

All of this reinforced Mattie's suspicions about Eloise Springfield as a possible candidate for her mother, but somehow the idea didn't feel right. She had a much stronger attachment to the notion that Miss Lily Martin might be her mother. Somehow Mattie felt a greater affinity for the petite and retiring librarian than for the tall and striking architect.

But Lily Martin was never mentioned in the society column as having gone away to college with Josh and Richard.

That didn't mean they wouldn't have helped her if she had called on them for help, but the likelihood would have been greater if she attended college near them. One of her priorities, Mattie decided, was to learn where Lily Martin had gotten her undergraduate degree.

By the time she had finished going through the papers published just prior to her birth and a few months beyond, she had to admit that she wasn't likely to find anything that would be helpful in her quest. Besides, her hands were black from the ink that had rubbed off the old newspapers, her nose was stuffy from the dust, and her stomach grumbled as though she hadn't eaten a huge breakfast at the Diner. Lunch, she decided, was next on the agenda, just as soon as she washed her hands.

Jeffry was seated behind his desk when she returned to the front of the building. He stood when he saw her. "Find anything of interest?" he asked.

Fortunately, a few facts from old front pages had struck her fancy, and she was able to cite a couple of interesting occurrences, such as the year the local high school football team won the state championship in its division.

Mattie thanked the editor for his cooperation, then headed off for lunch at Jill's Soup Bowl. She really wanted to lend what support she could to Jill's new business.

Apparently Mattie wasn't the only person who'd had that notion. The restaurant was so crowded that a line had formed outside the door. Mattie decided she was entirely too hungry to wait for a seat to open up so instead of eating at Jill's, she would return to the B and B, impose on Mrs. Dunmore for a sandwich, and then work on her article for the remainder of the afternoon.

By the time Mattie had organized her notes and begun writing, she had grown enthused about her topic and, as she often did, she lost herself in the work. By the time she stopped, it was almost six o'clock. She would have to hurry to shower, dress, and get back to the cottage in time for Denver and her to get to Beth Ann's by seven.

She made it by the skin of her teeth, pulling in behind Denver's car on Potter Street at 6:54. She grabbed her purse and exited the car, just as Denver stepped out on the front porch.

"You must have been watching for me," Mattie said as she rounded the back of her car.

"Yep. I was anxious to hear if you discovered anything of interest at the newspaper."

"Not much, I'm afraid. I'll fill you in on what little I learned after dinner. I'm sorry I'm running so late. I got caught up in my article and time got away from me."

"No problem." Denver jogged down the steps and offered Mattie his arm. "I just finished getting ready myself. Once Dallas got his hands on me, he dragged me to every house in the county he's bought for restoration. I didn't realize there were so many. And some of them are really great houses. One I especially like is called 'the old Masterson place.' We can visit a couple of them some time if you'd like."

Mattie switched her purse to her left hand and took Denver's arm. "Sure. I love going through old houses. Is Dallas thinking about security for all of them?"

"To some extent. He's been pretty surprised that people are so set on having security built in as he renovates. But as I pointed out to him, the people who are buying these places as summer homes probably live in gated communities and have no conception of how crime-free the town and county are up here."

"You're probably right. So what is he going to do?"

Before Denver could answer, they rounded the corner and approached Dallas' and Beth Ann's house. The front door swung open and Trevor stepped outside, a wide grin on his face. His arms were wrapped around little Matthew, who had a fist crammed in his mouth. Matthew's other hand rested on Trevor's face.

Trevor hurried to their side, his grin widening. "Hi Uncle Denver. Hi, Miss Meadows. Mom said I could bring Matthew out to say hello but he has to go to bed soon."

Matthew twisted in Trevor's arms and reached for Denver, who immediately grasped Matthew under the arms and raised him high into the air. The baby gurgled and waved his arms.

"Hi, little fellow," Denver said, lowering his arms and pulling the baby close against his chest. "I see you're already dressed in your pajamas."

Trevor answered for his half brother. "Yep. Our Mom insists on him getting to bed at a decent hour. Just like she always did when I was little." He wrinkled his nose.

"It doesn't seem to have hurt you," Denver noted. "You've grown up to be a healthy looking young man."

Trevor's blush and shy smile spoke of his appreciation for Denver's comment, but before he could respond, Dallas stepped out onto the wide, wrap-around porch.

"Beth Ann sent me to look for you folks. And to make sure Denver wasn't making off with his nephew."

Denver grinned and held Matthew just a bit tighter. "Hey, can I help it because the kid has discriminating taste and is partial to his uncle Denver?"

Dallas laughed. "If you'd been here at three o'clock this morning, I would have been tempted to give him to you."

"Ah ha!" Denver held Matthew at arm's length and addressed his next remarks to the baby. "Giving your old man a hard time, were you? Way to go, kid."

The front door swung open again, and Beth Ann stepped onto the porch. She was dressed simply in blue jeans and a short-sleeved cotton shirt and had pulled her hair into a ponytail, but she was still gorgeous. She plopped her hands on her hips. "Honestly! Here we have four men, counting Matthew, and I'll bet not a one of you has invited Mattie into the house." Her glare encompassed them all, but it was immediately followed by a smile. "Mattie, come with me. Dallas, you and Trevor take Matthew up and tuck him in. Denver, come help me carry the dishes to the dining room table."

Within seconds, everyone scattered to follow Beth Ann's orders. Mattie, who had been standing back and enjoying the banter, silently followed Beth Ann into the house, through the large entrance hall and down a wide hallway to the back of the house.

The kitchen boasted state-of-the-art appliances, granite countertops, and a tile floor. A bottle of wine sitting on the counter had been opened to breathe, and a large tossed salad sat on the bar in what appeared to be a hand-carved wooden bowl surrounded by smaller wooden bowls. Matching tongs completed the set.

Beth Ann smiled at Mattie. "If you don't mind, I'll let you dish up the salads while Denver carries the chicken pot pie to the dining room." She nodded toward the large casserole dish sitting on the stove and then tossed a couple of hot pot pads to Denver. He grabbed the pads as they flew toward him, then stepped over to the stove, picked up the dish, and exited through a door to the far side of the kitchen.

Mattie picked up the tongs and stood gazing at them a few seconds.

"Something wrong?" Beth Ann asked.

"I was just admiring these tongs. Did the same person carve both these and the bowls?"

"Yes, that would be Jeffrey Martin. His work is in tremendous demand, and there's a waiting list for everything he does. Fortunately for me, he's one of the artists who participates in the co-op I help run downtown, and he gave Dallas and me that salad set for a wedding present. I could never have afforded it otherwise."

"I can see why. It's beautiful. But I didn't realize you were part of a co-op. Maybe I should visit that and include it in my story about Barbourville."

"You won't get any objection from me. The publicity would be wonderful."

"Great! How about tomorrow?"

Denver and Dallas stepped into the kitchen together. "How about tomorrow for what?" Denver asked.

Beth Ann glanced at Denver. "I'll tell you while we eat. Help Mattie set the salads at each place while Dallas pours our wine. I need to run upstairs and kiss my baby before he goes to sleep."

Ten minutes later they were seated around the table and each had been served a plate of chicken pot pie. Salads were dressed and the wine had been poured. "Okay," Denver said, looking at Mattie. "What's on the agenda for tomorrow?"

Mattie took a sip of her wine and set her glass back down. "I had just asked Beth Ann if I could visit the co-op tomorrow."

"That would be fine," Beth Ann said, "except we're closed on Tuesdays. It's usually a slow business day. Besides, you already have an invitation for tomorrow."

"I do?" Mattie asked.

"Yes. Judge McCray stopped by here today looking for you. I didn't know where you were but I told him I'd pass along a message when you came to dinner tonight. Seems that Miss Evelyn is feeling much better and has invited all of us to lunch tomorrow."

"Me too?" Trevor had been sulking a bit because he'd been given milk to drink instead of the soda he preferred but he now looked up with a bright gleam in his eyes.

"Sorry, dear, but tomorrow's a school day," Beth Ann said.

Trevor's face grew longer. "Are they having a cook-out?"

"No, not this time. The judge claims that Dogwood winter is on its way and that the temperature will be too cold to cook outside tomorrow."

A frown touched Dallas' brow. "I listened to the weather report today and nothing was mentioned about a cold front."

Beth Ann shrugged. "You can choose to listen to the weatherman, or you can choose to listen to the judge, but personally, I'd take a jacket to work with me tomorrow if I were you."

She turned to smile at Mattie. "Do you have Dogwood winter where you're from, Mattie?"

"Occasionally, yes, but it's usually rather mild in Georgia."

"You're lucky, then. At this altitude, Dogwood winter

can be downright cold. In fact, I've known us to have snow flurries this late in April before."

"I wish I'd brought some heavier clothes with me in that case," Mattie said. "But I'm sure I can make do."

The rest of the evening passed quickly. Dinner was a relaxed affair with lots of chatter. Following dinner, Mattie and Denver helped Beth Ann load the dishwasher while Trevor washed the pots and pans and Dallas dried. Afterwards Trevor excused himself to go to his room and the adults adjourned to the parlor to visit for a while longer.

Beth Ann sat on the sofa and pulled her feet up under her. She motioned for Denver for sit opposite her and Mattie beside her. Dallas took a chair next to his brother.

Beth Ann looked at Denver. "Dallas tells me he was picking your brain about security today. Have you learned enough working with your friend to be able to envision what Dallas will need to do to satisfy the city folks who are interested in buying houses around here?"

Denver nodded. "I think so. I learned about some of the newer technology in Jacksonville, and the rest I'd already picked up working with Steve. So, yes, I think I gave him some good pointers."

"That's great." She turned to Mattie. "And how did your day go today? I understand you were looking into the town's history."

Mattie had ended up doing much more research into the town's past than her own, so she was able to answer honestly. "I went through a lot of back copies of the newspaper and found some interesting tidbits that I was able to work into my story."

"You've already started writing it?" Beth Ann asked.

"Yes, I spent the rest of the afternoon working on my laptop at the B and B. The story's going well but I still have room to include more information about the town. That's one reason I'll be around a few more days."

Beth Ann grinned. "That's great. I look forward to seeing more of you."

By nine, Mattie decided it was time to leave. She knew the following day was a workday for Dallas, and she didn't want to keep him up too late.

So she stood, announced that she had to go, and thanked Beth Ann and Dallas for a lovely evening. Denver also stood and said he would see that Mattie got back to her lodging safely. Ten minutes later, they had strolled back to the cottage.

Mattie paused on the sidewalk leading to the front porch. "You really don't have to follow me to the B and B tonight."

Denver's silence was his response.

Mattie smiled, more pleased than she would have expected. "I won't argue if that's what you want to do."

He nodded. "Would you like to come in for a cup of coffee? There's something I've been meaning to ask you."

"Sure." For Mattie, the night was still young, and she welcomed a reason to delay going back to the B and B.

Denver had left lights burning in the cottage, so they

easily made their way to the kitchen where Denver started a pot of decaf brewing.

Mattie got the cups and saucers from the cupboard and retrieved one of her favorite creams from the refrigerator before seating herself at the table and waiting for Denver to do the same.

"What do you have on your schedule for tomorrow?" she asked while waiting for the coffee to brew.

Denver leaned back against the cabinet. "I'm hoping we can go to the library again. Isn't Miss Martin supposed to be there tomorrow?"

"Yes, and I'm glad you're still interested in helping me. Oh! I was going to tell you about what little I found in the newspapers." She gave him a quick overview of the society columns she'd read.

"Not much there," Denver commented. He straightened, then turned to look at the coffee maker. "Great, it's ready." He poured each of them a cup and carried both to the table.

Mattie thanked him and reached for her cream. "The frequent references to Elaine Smithfield traveling with Josh and Richard was the only possible clue, but for some reason, I just can't imagine her getting pregnant and giving her child up for adoption."

Denver frowned. "Keep in mind, she was just a girl then, not the sophisticated and educated woman she is now."

"True," Mattie agreed, "but still, it just doesn't feel right to me."

"Is it my imagination, or are you leaning toward Lily Martin?"

Mattie sighed. "I'm not sure. She seems more the type. That is, of course, assuming that I know what the type is."

"I don't follow."

"I'm going on the assumption that a woman who would give her child up for adoption is one who is a bit shy and retiring. But I don't have any basis at all for that opinion. It's just me projecting my own feelings onto other people. I know that's not what I should be doing."

"We can't always make our feelings follow logic, I've discovered." Denver grimaced. "My own brothers always considered me a bit strange because I prefer a routine rather than excitement and change. But back to Miss Martin, maybe when we see her at the library tomorrow, you'll be able to refine your feelings a bit more."

"Maybe," Mattie allowed. "But enough about me. You said you had something to ask me."

"Right. It's about this Raynaud's Disease. We got interrupted when you were telling me about it. If I understood correctly, you hope your Raynaud's Disease is hereditary. What difference does it make?"

Mattie centered her coffee cup on her saucer, then squared her shoulders and looked up to meet Denver's curious gaze. "According to my research, if the condition is hereditary, it's only a nuisance to most people. If it *isn't* hereditary, it can be an early symptom of much more serious conditions such as lupus. So you see, if I can ascertain that my case is hereditary, I'll have much less to worry about."

Denver reached across the table and placed his hand on top of hers. "No wonder you feel this sense of urgency. Anyone would, I suspect. I don't know how much help I can be, but I'm sure willing to try."

"You mean you'll stay on in Barbourville a couple more days?"

"I've got a couple more weeks before I'm due back in Chicago. How long can you stick around?"

"I don't have anything pressing back at home," Mattie said. "Even my article on Potter Place isn't due for another month, so I can stick around as long as need be."

Denver's smile was broad. "Great! In that case, I'd better escort you home so we can get to the library at a decent hour in the morning. We'll need to finish there and get to the judge's house in plenty of time for lunch."

"Oh, that's right. I'd almost forgotten about lunch." Mattie pushed back from the table and stood. "Let's wash up these dishes and then I'll go."

"No need to help with that. I'll stack them in the sink and do them tomorrow afternoon."

"If you're sure," Mattie said, frowning. "I don't like to leave you with all the chores to do."

"I've got nothing pressing right now except helping you, so don't worry about it. If you're ready, I'll follow you to the B and B in my car."

A smile lifted the corners of Mattie's lips. "I won't waste my breath trying to change your mind."

"Great." Denver stepped around the table and reached for Mattie's hand. She placed her palm in his, expecting him to lead her toward the front of the cottage. Instead, he gently pulled her toward him, giving her plenty of time to back away if she wished.

She didn't wish. In fact, Mattie looked forward to another kiss from Denver. She had enjoyed his earlier embrace, especially considering the unprecedented feeling of both excitement and contentment that had inundated her senses. She couldn't help wondering if she would feel the same this time.

Denver captured her gaze, his eyes widening slightly when he realized that Mattie was leaning toward him in anticipation of his next move.

A smile brightened his eyes, and his gaze continued to hold Mattie's as their lips touched gently.

Mattie's eyelids drifted shut as Denver deepened the kiss. Somehow she hadn't expected this from him, this ability to send sparks racing through her veins until the tips of her toes tingled.

It was wonderful and, at the same time, a tiny bit frightening. The last thing Mattie needed was to fall for Denver Vance, who would be going home to his life and career in Chicago in a few days.

She pulled back gently, and he released her, although his reluctance was almost palpable. Even then, when he no longer had his arms wrapped around her, his hands rested on her arms just above her elbows.

"Am I moving too quickly?" he asked.

Mattie sighed. "I won't lie to you, Denver. I enjoy being with you. I enjoy your kisses, and I love the feeling I experience in your arms."

Denver's sigh echoed hers. "Obviously there's a 'but' at the end of your sentence."

She nodded. "In a few days you'll be headed north and I'll be headed south. There's no reason for us to start something that will only make both of us sad when we part."

"Too late," Denver said. "I'll already be sad when we go our separate ways. But good-byes don't have to be forever. We have cell phones and landlines and e-mail. We could continue to stay in touch."

Mattie knew that neither e-mails nor phone calls would be enough for either of them, but she didn't want to force the issue now. She wanted to enjoy Denver's company as long as possible.

So she smiled. "Okay. But let's take it slow, all right?"

Denver grinned. "All right. And just so you know, I plan to kiss you good night when I walk you to the door at the Dunmore's in a few minutes."

Mattie returned his grin. "And just so you know, that's exactly what I was hoping for when I decided not to object to your escorting me back this evening."

Denver's grin widened. "Shall we go then?"

"Let's," Mattie responded, and they left the cottage together.

Eight

The instant that Mattie awoke the next morning, she knew Judge McCray had been right about the advent of Dogwood winter. Clearly a cold wave had descended upon McCray County, and the air in her bedroom had chilled so much that she had unconsciously curled into a tight ball during the night in an effort to keep warm.

She clenched her teeth and straightened her cramped legs, then immediately drew them back up next to her body. The bed coverings that had not been warmed by her body felt frigid against her legs.

Mattie grasped the bottom of her sleep shirt and pulled it down over her knees. The temporary warmth contributed little toward her comfort and she realized there was no way to get warm unless she got out of bed long enough to hunt more cover.

By now, she was so wide awake, she had no hope of going back to sleep. Besides, the idea of a hot shower was enticing enough to have her throwing back the blanket and jumping up. Just as her feet hit the floor, a loud clunking from the basement level suggested that Jack Dunmore had fired up the furnace.

"Thank goodness," Mattie murmured. She grabbed her robe from the foot of the bed, wrapped it around her, and picked up her travel alarm, which also recorded the room temperature.

"Sixty-four. No wonder I'm freezing." She set the clock back down and hurried into the bathroom where she could turn on the overhead heater. She knew from experience that the bath would soon be cozy, and the hot steam from her shower would add to the comfort of the room. Maybe by the time she had to go back into the bedroom, the furnace would have warmed the house up a little bit.

Half an hour later, Mattie gingerly cracked the bathroom door and eased into her bedroom. The furnace had begun to do its job, and the air was no longer chilled, although it was still far from comfortable.

She hurried to the closet to search out the warmest clothes she'd brought with her. Unfortunately, she hadn't been thinking of Dogwood winter when she left home, so her warmest clothes consisted of jeans and a sweatshirt, which simply wouldn't do for a visit to the judge's house for lunch.

She finally decided on her black cotton slacks, a long-sleeved ivory blouse, and her tan sweater. It wasn't her most attractive outfit, but at least she'd have on two sets of long sleeves.

Twenty minutes later, she stuck her head out into the hallway and inhaled the odors drifting up from Carmen Dunmore's kitchen. She couldn't decide which smelled most enticing, the coffee or the sausage. Fortunately, Carmen liked for her guests to eat hearty, so Mattie knew she'd receive a warm welcome when she made her way down to the dining room.

By the time she'd finished breakfast, the temperature in the house had climbed into the comfort zone. She hated the thoughts of going outside into the chill again, but at the same time, she looked forward to seeing Denver.

A smile tugged at the corners of her lips. Their good night kiss last evening when he'd walked her to the door had filled her with such exhilaration that she couldn't wait to see him again, to feel the warmth of his touch, to hear the sound of his voice.

She was perfectly aware that her behavior was as silly as any schoolgirl, but she didn't care. Denver was a joy to be around, and she was looking forward to spending the day with him.

She was convinced he felt the same about her, especially when, twenty minutes later, she pulled up in front of the cottage and he immediately opened the front door and stepped outside to greet her.

He hurried down the porch steps, a wide grin on his

face. "Good morning," he called as he rounded the front of the car and hurried to open her door. "Are you about to freeze to death this morning?"

Mattie returned his grin. "At least I'm not worried about suffering from a heat stroke." She swung her feet out of the car and stood. "Judge McCray was certainly right about Dogwood winter, wasn't he?"

"He sure was. Do you want to warm up by coming inside and having a cup of coffee?"

Mattie glanced at her watch. "Thanks anyway, but I don't want to take the time. The library opens around ten, which is only half an hour from now. Would you mind if we walked? Mrs. Dunmore provided such an excellent breakfast this morning that I overate and need to work off some of the calories."

"No problem. Just come inside long enough for me to turn off the coffee and grab a jacket."

Mattie nodded and walked ahead of him to the porch. "I'd like to come inside for a few minutes as research for my article. I should be able to report how the cottage feels when the temperature drops suddenly. That's the type of information that the editor of *Cottage Vacations* wants me to include."

"I think you'll be impressed with the comfort level. The furnace kicked on during the night and the temperature inside was just about right when I got out of bed this morning."

"Lucky you," Mattie muttered. Still, she was glad to

hear that the cottage remained comfortable even when the weather changed quickly.

She was also thankful to get out of the chilly air for a few minutes when she stepped into the entrance hall. "Wow, this is cozy," she said.

"You can warm up while I go upstairs to get my jacket. And if you don't mind, step in the kitchen and set the coffee off the warmer."

"Sure." Mattie hurried down the hall but paused in the kitchen doorway to admire the way the morning sun shown through the windows and illuminated the piece of stained glass hanging above the sink. The colorful image of pink dogwood blossoms reminded her that spring was in full bloom despite the chill in the air.

The smell of overheated coffee attracted her attention. Only a thin layer of coffee coated the bottom of the carafe, so she moved it onto a trivet to cool and turned the warmer off. It was just as well that she didn't plan to ingest more caffeine, she decided. She already felt unusually jittery today. She rolled her shoulders and stretched, trying to relieve a bit of the tension.

She was still stretching when Denver stepped into the room. He carried a burnt orange jacket over his arm. Mattie felt some of the tension draining from her shoulders when his lips curved into a lazy smile.

"I'm good at massages," he said. "Interested?"

Mattie grinned. "Tempting, but no thanks. I want to get to the library as soon as possible. We need to finish there in time to go to the judge's house for lunch. Where does he live, do you know?"

Denver's smile faded. "I have no idea. Probably nearby. I've noticed that all of the McCrays live within a few blocks of each other. We'll ask Miss Martin at the library."

"Good idea. Ready?"

"Yep. Let's go."

Their walk toward the library took them through town, past Beth Ann's Place, which wasn't open for business yet, and past Sonny's Diner, where people had spilled out onto the street while waiting for a table to become vacant.

Half a dozen people spoke to Denver, and most nodded to Mattie. A few shot disapproving glances at her, and she suspected those people had mistaken Denver for Dallas and thought that Mattie was in the company of a married man. She made a mental note to warn Beth Ann that some of the townspeople might drop a hint to her about seeing Dallas with another woman. Of course she didn't figure Beth Ann was going to worry. The slowest intellect could see that Dallas was crazy about Beth Ann.

"You're awfully quiet," Denver commented. They had passed through the center of town and now walked along the sidewalk leading to the library. "Worried about seeing Miss Martin?"

Mattie shook her head. "Not at all. In fact, I wasn't even thinking about her, but I suppose I should be giving some thought as to how I'm going to handle our visit to the library. Since I already know that Miss Marshall's history of the county is checked out, what excuse do I have for coming by this morning?"

Ignoring her question, Denver reached to grasp Mattie's hand, then pulled her to a stop in front of a stone house with a discrete business sign in the front yard. "McCray and Smithfield, Architects," he read aloud. "I didn't realize that Richard and Eloise had offices in an old house on Kessler Boulevard. This is a great location."

"It sure is. And that looks like Eloise's vehicle coming down the street now."

Denver turned to look at the approaching SUV. "It is. I recognize her car from the cookout. I admired it when she pulled up in front of Dallas' and Beth Ann's house."

The vehicle turned into the narrow driveway, then slowed to a stop. Eloise rolled down her window and smiled. "Good morning, folks. Were you looking for either me or Richard?"

Denver answered. "No, we're on our way to the library and were just passing by when I noticed your sign in the yard. Neither Mattie nor I realized you and Richard had offices here."

"It's a beautiful old house," Mattie noted.

Eloise's smile broadened. "It is. Would you like to come in and look around?"

Mattie glanced at her watch, then nodded. "I'd love to. Old houses are one of my passions."

"Then you'll enjoy seeing inside," Eloise told her. "When Richard and I renovated the house, we were careful to retain all of the original architectural features that made it unique. If you'll go to the front door, I'll park around back and come through the house to let you in."

"Great," Mattie said, then turned to Denver. "Do you mind?"

"Of course not. I'd like to see the inside. I live in an older house myself, you know."

"Oh, that's right." Mattie tightened her grasp on his hand. Her earlier tension had disappeared and despite the day's gloomy weather, she felt as though the sun had broken through the clouds. "Let's go." She tugged on his hand. They walked up the brick sidewalk and paused on the front porch. A few seconds later, Eloise opened the door for them and stepped back so they could come inside.

The entrance hall had been painted a soft cream color in an attempt to lighten the small space, which had no natural light because the front door was solid oak. A staircase was situated to the left. To the right, a door led into a room Eloise and Richard clearly used for a reception area.

"Richard and I had to do a great deal of work when we first bought this place," Eloise said. "It had been a rental house for a number of years and then had been divided up into four apartments. The damage was extensive, but we managed to reclaim most of the original woodwork."

She motioned for them to step into the reception area and allowed them a minute to examine the beautifully carved crown molding and mantel. Chair molding divided the wall into two horizontal spaces that had been painted two shades of blue. "This was originally the parlor," she said. "As you can see, we furnished it with study modern furniture since we didn't want our customers feeling that they were sitting on flimsy antiques. Richard, however, found some fantastic old furniture for his office, which I can't show you because he isn't in yet and we respect each other's privacy. However, I'm free to show you my space."

"We'd love to see your office," Mattie said, aware that she could speak both for herself and for Denver. She'd noticed his careful examination of the woodwork and realized that he appreciated the craftsmanship that was a holdover from decades earlier.

Eloise turned and led them back into the hall, past the staircase, and into a room that had originally been the dining room. Windows on the outside wall looked out over a brick patio with wrought iron benches and tables situated under the overhanging maple limbs. Corner columns were topped by concrete flower pots filled with masses of purple pansies.

"I love my view," Eloise said. "And I love to fill the patio in the summer with pots of annuals. When the weather becomes too hot for the pansies, I put Dragon Wing Begonias in my planters on the columns. They flourish there, and I enjoy them until frost."

"It's gorgeous," Mattie said. Her gaze swept the room, taking in the muted Persian carpet, the antique writing desk sitting in a corner, and the old-fashioned sideboard on which sat a sleek black coffee maker. Centering the room was a huge U-shaped workstation of gleaming cherry. Computers sat on either side of the U, complete with various components including multiple screens, a color laser printer, a copier, and a fax machine.

"Whoa," Denver murmured. "Great work space. You could easily have several projects going at once."

Eloise nodded. "That's exactly what I do. I work best when I can switch back and forth between jobs. Would either of you care for a cup of coffee? Our secretary is taking today off, but I can put a pot on to brew."

"None for me, thanks," Denver murmured, his gaze still riveted on Eloise's state-of-the-art workstation.

"I'll pass, too," Mattie said. "We'd better be going. We're on our way to the library to research county history, and then we're invited to the judge's house for lunch. Are you going to be there?"

"Certainly. I'd never pass up an invitation to Bob and Evelyn's house for a meal. Evelyn is a fantastic cook, and they love having guests."

"I hope she isn't pushing herself," Mattie said. "I had understood from Judge McCray that his wife was under the weather."

"Apparently it was just one of those twenty-four-hour bugs," Eloise said. "I'm sure Evelyn wouldn't be inviting guests if she thought she might be contagious."

Denver finally looked up from his perusal of Eloise's computer components. "By the way, we realized this morning that we don't know where Judge McCray lives. Is it in this neighborhood?"

Eloise's eyebrows shot up. "I can't believe no one thought to tell you. Of course we're all so familiar with this county that we probably assume everybody else knows their way around. But no, the judge doesn't live in town at all. His and Evelyn's home is about ten miles from here. They live on the old McCray home place, which was a working farm for many years. If you're not familiar with the county, it can be a little difficult to find because some of the roads aren't marked. Just a minute and I'll draw you a map."

Eloise stepped behind her desk and sat down in the large leather executive chair. She opened a desk drawer and pulled out a piece of stationery. "Who will be driving?"

Denver glanced at Mattie. "I will," he said.

"Then if you'll step around here beside me, I'll explain what the landmarks are as I draw the map."

Mattie took the opportunity to inspect the room's antiques while Denver and Eloise were going over directions to the judge's house. She didn't consider herself an expert, but she certainly knew quality when she saw it, and she was especially impressed with the old writing desk in the corner, which led her to the conclusion that she really should start a savings account just for the purchase of such a desk should she ever come across one for sale.

Her thoughts returned to the present when Denver stepped back around Eloise's desk with a sheet of paper in his hand. "I shouldn't have any trouble finding the house with these directions," he said. He handed the paper to Mattie. "Do you mind putting this in your purse until we start to lunch?"

"Not at all." Mattie reached for the paper and was instantly aware that she was holding a high quality piece of vellum rather than the traditional bond that most office stationery was printed on. She glanced down at the letterhead and saw that it was imprinted with Eloise's name rather than the firm's name. Not many people in this day and age went so far as to have their personal stationery printed on such high quality paper, and Mattie's regard for this very elegant woman increased a couple of notches. She folded the sheet in half and slid it into her purse.

"I'll look forward to visiting with both of you some more at lunch today," Eloise said. Her smile was sincere but her words were obviously a gentle dismissal.

"We'd better be on our way," Mattie said quickly.

"Thanks for the directions," Denver added. "We'll see you in a couple of hours."

Eloise walked them to the front door. When she opened it, a rush of cold air greeted them. "I do believe it's turned even cooler," she commented. "The cold front must be moving more quickly than predicted."

Mattie shivered. "You're right. I definitely think it's turning colder." She started buttoning her jacket. "Thank you for the tour, Eloise. The house is lovely."

"You're welcome, my dear." Eloise wrapper her arms around herself. "Goodness, but that wind has picked up. I hate to see you walking in this weather. Can I give you a ride to the library?"

"We'll warm up as soon as we start walking," Mattie said, aware that Eloise probably needed to start her workday. "Thanks anyway." She thrust her hands into her pockets, then waited for Denver to fall into step beside her as they headed down the brick sidewalk toward Kessler Boulevard.

As soon as they stepped out of the shelter of the old shrubbery lining the architects' yard and onto the sidewalk leading toward the library, a particularly vicious burst of wind slammed into them, nearly pushing Mattie off her feet. She was thankful to feel Denver's arm wrap around her waist to steady her.

"I'm walking with you to the library," Denver announced. "Then I'm going back to the cottage to get my car. There's no need for you to be out in this wind any more than necessary."

Mattie wasn't inclined to argue with him, but she hated the thought of him walking back to the cottage through the increasing chill of the day. After all, it had been her idea to walk this morning. "Why don't you call Dallas to pick you up?"

"He's probably out on a job site this morning. I'll call the sheriff and if he's not busy, he'll come and get me."

"Okay." Mattie kept forgetting that Denver was related to the sheriff through his niece. "Do you think he'll mind?"

"Knowing Daniel, he'll see it as part of his duties. I've never seen a man who takes his responsibilities any more seriously."

"Well I sure hope he's not busy. This wind seems to be growing colder by the second, and neither of us is dressed for winter-like conditions."

"Don't worry about me. If Daniel's busy, I'll just call Megan or Beth Ann. Let's concentrate on getting to the library without getting blown away."

Denver's arm tightened around her as another gust slammed into them. Mattie ducked her head and bent into the wind, struggling to stay on her feet, even with Denver's support.

She had given up trying to talk. The wind would have ripped the words from her mouth anyway, but she was tremendously thankful for Denver's supporting arm. She couldn't imagine trying to walk into the blasts of frigid air without him by her side.

Suddenly the wind slowed, just as a vehicle pulled up beside them.

"It's Eloise," Denver said. "She's rolling her window down."

Mattie turned to look at the vehicle. Sure enough, Eloise Smithfield was motioning to them. "Get in," she called out the window. "I'm driving you to the library. You'll both catch your deaths in this weather."

"Thanks," Denver said. "Let's go, Mattie."

"Sounds wonderful," Mattie said. She climbed into the front seat and sank back against the soft upholstery. "This is really nice of you, Eloise. I can't believe how cold it's gotten so quickly."

"That happens sometimes at this elevation," Eloise said. She reached to turn her heater up a notch. "I wouldn't have let you leave if I'd known how cold the weather was turning. When I stepped outside to water the pansies, I realized that the temperature was falling rapidly. I hope you don't plan to walk back to the cottage after you finish at the library."

Mattie, who had been holding her hands in front of the warm air streaming from the heater vent, spoke up quickly. "Actually, I'm hoping you'll drop me off at the library and take Denver back to the cottage. Then he can drive back to the library and pick me up in time for us to get to the judge's house for lunch."

Denver, who had crawled into the back seat after helping Mattie into the front, now leaned forward. "If it's an imposition, I'll call Daniel or Megan or—"

"It's no imposition at all," Eloise said immediately. "It's just half a dozen blocks. I insist on taking you."

"Thanks. I appreciate it." Denver leaned back in his seat.

Before Mattie had a chance to speak again, Eloise was pulling up in front of Moser Memorial Library. The small brick building sat back from the road several feet and a semicircular sidewalk led from the street and back again.

Mattie opened her door. "Thanks so much," she said, then realized that Denver was waiting to help her down. When she stepped out onto the sidewalk, he gave her a quick peck on the cheek.

"Whoa! Your face is cold. Hurry inside. I'll come in and find you when I get back." Then he climbed into the front seat with Eloise and waved to Mattie. She waved back, then reached to touch her cheek where Denver's warm lips had settled for a second. She really should call a halt to whatever was growing between them, but at the same time, she had never felt this wonderful and exciting sense of anticipation with any other man. She thoroughly enjoyed being around Denver, and while common sense warned her that their relationship would be short lived, she didn't want it to end any sooner than necessary.

She watched Eloise's SUV turn a corner and disappear from view. She sighed, then squared her shoulders and turned her back on the wind. She needed to push Denver to the back of her mind for the moment and concentrate on her upcoming interview with the local librarian, a woman who could also be her birth mother.

NINE

By the time Mattie stepped into the shelter of the library's entrance, she was chilled to the bone. She stopped just inside the door and stood quietly, looking around and soaking up the warmth pouring from the registers.

For a minute she thought she was the only patron in the library that morning. Then she spotted an elderly man seated at one of the tables and leafing through a magazine. She looked toward the check-out counter, expecting to see Lily Martin. Instead, a young woman Mattie had never seen before looked up and flashed a welcoming smile.

Mattie returned the smile and walked over to the counter.

"Good morning," the young woman said. "I'm Jessica Foster. Can I help you?"

"I hope so. I dropped by yesterday to see Miss Martin and was told she had gone to Knoxville but would be back today. Is she in?"

"Oh, I'm sorry. She was in first thing this morning, but she left a few minutes ago to take our overdue notices to the post office. Then she was going to the office supply store to buy an ink cartridge and then to Judge McCray's house for lunch. I don't expect her back until this afternoon. Can I give her a message for you?"

Mattie forced a smile. "No, thank you. I'll be seeing her at Judge McCray's house. But I'm waiting for a ride so if you don't mind, I'll just sit over near the front windows where I can watch the street."

"By all means. There are some current magazines on the racks near the door if you want to glance through one while waiting."

Mattie nodded her thanks and walked over to racks where she selected a news magazine and then took a seat near the front. Looking out, she saw dark gray clouds rolling in, quickly blotting out any remaining patches of blue sky. Wind continued to whip the tender leaves on the willows outside the window, and a few flecks of snow twirled about in the gusts.

Mattie shivered at the thought of stepping out into that arctic blast, but at least she would only have to walk from the library to Denver's car rather than all the way back to the cottage where her car was still parked.

"I wonder if Beth Ann would loan me a coat," she murmured to herself. "Or tell me where I could buy one." Beth Ann's Place had once been a clothing store, she had learned, before Beth Ann turned it into a co-op featuring the creations of local artists.

A flicker of movement drew Mattie's attention to the street outside. Denver's dark gray Mercedes had just pulled up to the curb. Mattie returned her magazine to the rack and headed for the front door.

She dashed down the sidewalk and motioned for Denver to stay inside his vehicle. Head down, she hurried to the passenger's side and didn't look up until the door popped open from inside.

Denver had leaned across the front seat to let her in. Now he straightened and then reached to turn the heater up another notch.

"Can you believe this weather?" Mattie asked. She clambered into her seat, fastened her seat belt, and leaned forward to revel in the hot air blowing from the vents. "If anyone had told me yesterday that it could turn this cold this quickly, I wouldn't have believed them."

"I'm hoping it can turn warm just as fast," Denver said. "How did your meeting with Miss Martin go?"

"I missed her again, but I did learn that she'll be at Judge McCray's house for lunch today."

"Sounds as though you're going to have more luck finding her outside the library than in," Denver commented. "Speaking of lunch, is it too early to head to the judge's house, do you think?"

Mattie glanced at the clock on the dash. "I don't think so. We should allow extra time in case we get lost."

"Good idea." Denver looked out the rear window to make sure nothing was coming and then pulled back out into the street. "Do you have the map Eloise drew for us?"

"Just a sec." Mattie opened her purse and pulled the directions out. She studied the map a minute. "Let's see now. Okay. We're supposed to head out of town on highway one-fifty-seven."

"How do we get from Kessler Boulevard to highway one-fifty-seven?"

"Just go straight. Kessler turns into one-fifty-seven."

"Okay." Denver grinned. "You look good with wind-tossed hair."

Mattie immediately pulled down the visor and flipped up the small door covering the mirror. "Thanks for telling me. I don't want to visit the judge's house looking like a tumbleweed."

She ran her hand deep into her purse, pulled out a small brush, and started working on her hair. "What do you think of Eloise Smithfield as a candidate for my mother?"

"She certainly went out of her way to be nice to us this morning, but I'm not sure that proves anything. Maybe she treats everybody that way."

"Maybe," Mattie said. She turned her head, trying to get a better view in the small mirror. "But I really feel no sense of familiarity when I'm with her."

She dropped the hairbrush back into her bag and picked up the map again. "We should be coming to a crossroads soon with a white house on our right. We pass the house and turn right onto a paved road."

Denver slowed and made the turn. "What next?"

"Five miles straight on this road."

"Okay. Back to our discussion of Eloise Smithfield. Are you sure you would feel a sense of familiarity if you met your mother?"

"Of course I'm not sure, although I'd like to think so. I mean, a mother should seem familiar, shouldn't she?"

Denver frowned. "That would depend on the mother. Some would, but some wouldn't."

"I suppose you're right." Mattie sighed and flipped the visor back up. "I'd still like to think I'd feel something out of the ordinary though." She sat up a bit straighter. "Look at the car just ahead of us. Isn't that the sheriff's cruiser?"

"It sure is. I'd say we could follow him to the judge's house. That's got to be where he's heading."

"No doubt," Mattie agreed. She glanced again at the map Eloise had drawn. "Yes, he's turning next to a red brick house. Obviously he's on his way to his uncle's place." She folded the map and eased it into an outside pocket of her purse.

Five minutes later, Denver followed the sheriff's cruiser when it turned into a driveway leading to a large white farmhouse sitting under the canopy of spreading oak trees. The house, like the oaks around it, appeared to have spread out over the years. A wing had been added to the left of the original house, another to the right, and one even ran off at an angle with an enclosed breezeway connecting the new part to the old. Considering the additions, the house should have looked like a cobbled-up mess. Instead, it appeared down-to-earth and welcoming.

The driveway curved in front of the house and then took a sharp turn to the right, feeding into a large paved area under one of the largest of the trees. Denver pulled his car in beside the sheriff's cruiser, then glanced into his rear view mirror.

"Looks as though Eloise is coming in right behind us," he commented.

Mattie glanced back at the SUV. "Do you think it's strange that both Eloise and Lily are treated like members of the McCray family?"

"Can't say that I do," Denver responded with raised brows. "After all, they've all been friends for most of their lives. Besides, Eloise and Richard are business partners, and Josh and Lily appear to be sweethearts."

"You're right," Mattie said. "Sorry. I'm just a little nervous. I have this strange feeling that there's more to the judge's invitation than...well, just an invitation."

Denver frowned. "What do you mean?"

"Oh, I don't know. I'm being silly. Let's go, shall we?"

Denver gave her an encouraging smile and opened his car door. Almost immediately, a cold wind muscled its way inside the vehicle.

"Brrr." Mattie reached for her door handle, not willing to wait on Denver to come around and open it for her. She was eager to get inside the house and out of the cold.

Denver met her at the back of the car and nodded to the front porch. "The judge and Miss Evelyn are coming out to greet us."

Mattie followed his gaze. Sure enough, both their host and hostess now stood outside on the porch. The judge sported a wide and welcoming grin while Evelyn, dressed casually in a housedress and apron, threw up her hand in welcome. "Come on in," she called. "This wind is nasty today."

Mattie was eager to take Evelyn up on her invitation. The wind had grown into a steady, punishing stream of frigid air, and Mattie couldn't wait to get inside where she'd be protected from its unpleasant bite. She figured the temperature must have dropped into the forties, with a wind chill even lower, which would account for the familiar and unwelcome tingling sensation that had invaded the middle and ring fingers on both of her hands.

She took Denver's proffered arm, ducked her head, and hurried across the lawn and up the wooden steps to the front porch.

"Delighted to see you both," the judge said, slapping Denver on the back.

"So glad you could come, my dear," Evelyn said, giving Mattie a bright smile. "We'll go inside and get warm. Ah, but let's wait just a second on Eloise. She's getting out of her car now."

Mattie turned from greeting her hostess to watch Eloise

hurrying toward them. Denver and the judge also turned toward the front yard, and the judge called out a greeting to Eloise, who threw up a hand in acknowledgment. At least her hand was gloved, Mattie noticed, unlike her own. Eloise hurried up the porch steps and paused to smile and say hello to her host and hostess.

Seeing that the others on the porch were busy greeting Eloise, Mattie spread her fingers and glanced down at her hands. Sure enough, the four fingers that had started tingling when she stepped out of the car had now turned white, and the tingling sensation had given way to a feeling of numbness.

She quickly shrugged her handbag onto her shoulder and then clasped her hands together in front of her in hopes of warming the fingers enough to encourage blood flow to the tips. She looked up again just in time to catch Eloise and the judge glancing away from her hands and into each other's eyes. If they were surprised—and Mattie would have sworn that both were—neither said a word. The judge's slightly elevated brows and Eloise's minute tightening of her lips were the only signs that they had noticed Mattie's fingers and that her condition meant something to each of them.

Immediately Mattie looked into Denver's face, eager to see if he had noticed anything unusual in the behavior of the judge and Eloise, but he had turned to look toward the driveway and the small blue Toyota that was making its way toward them.

"Ah, here comes Lily," Eloise murmured. Her gaze cut quickly to Mattie and then back toward the car. "Who else are we expecting, Bob?"

Evelyn answered in place of her husband. "No one, my dear. Megan called and said one of the babies has the sniffles and she doesn't want to bring any of them out in this weather." She turned toward Daniel. "Do you think Megan needs any help? I'll be glad to baby sit with two of the girls if she needs to take little Brianna to the doctor."

The sheriff bent and kissed his hostess' chubby cheek. "You'll a doll, Aunt Evelyn, but Beth Ann already offered. They'll work it out between them."

"Okay, dear, but I expect you to take some food home with you when you leave so that Megan doesn't have to cook supper tonight. No doubt she has a cranky baby to contend with, so I don't want you making extra work for her."

"Yes, ma'am." The sheriff glanced at Mattie and gave her a quick wink and a smile, then turned back to his aunt. "If you say so, ma'am."

Evelyn grinned. "I say so." She turned to wave to Lily Martin who had now parked and was making her way across the yard. "Hurry, dear."

Within seconds, Lily had mounted the steps and joined the group gathered on the porch. She smiled and nodded to Mattie and Denver, then turned to the judge. "Heavens, Bob," she said. "You warned everybody that Dogwood winter was coming, but you didn't tell us it would be this fierce. I'm half frozen to death."

Evelyn spoke up immediately. "Let's all get inside where it's warm. Bob, my dear, will you open the door for us please?"

Mattie forced herself to smile as the men stepped back and waved the women toward the warmth that poured outside when the judge opened the door to the hallway of the old farmhouse. She strongly suspected that Judge McCray and Eloise had noticed the condition of her hands and that each had silently communicated a message to the other, but she couldn't be positive. Perhaps she had imagined their reaction. She wished she could talk to Denver but knew that was impossible until after the luncheon was behind them.

Lunch was served in the McCray's huge kitchen/dining area, which was located in the wing that had been added on most recently. A massive oak table in the dining area held all the ingredients necessary for making sandwiches, along with a variety of side dishes, including macaroni salad, potato salad, and slaw.

Mattie fell into step with the others as Evelyn gently herded her guests toward the table, but she stepped to one side when she spotted a brightly burning blaze in the large fireplace that graced an outside wall of the kitchen. She hurried over and held her hands out to the blaze in hopes that a few seconds of additional warmth would bring color back to her fingertips. She knew she couldn't continue to hide her hands when she joined the others at the table.

A few seconds later, Denver stepped up beside her. He glanced toward her hands, then turned sideways a bit in order to shield her from the others. Catching her eye, he nodded his understanding of her predicament and held his own hands out to the fire.

Aware that he was doing all he could to keep the others from thinking that her actions were anything out of the ordinary, Mattie smiled her thanks. She continued to hold her hands in the warmth emanating from the blaze, and soon tingling sensations replaced the numbness in her fingers and color slowly edged toward the tips.

"Thank goodness," Mattie murmured to Denver. "I'm ready to join the others now." She started when she realized that the judge now stood on her other side. She hadn't heard him approach.

"Nothing like a nice, warm fire on a cold day," the judge said. His tone was jovial, and a bright smile lifted the corners of his mouth, but Mattie felt sure she detected a calculating glint in his eyes. She immediately dropped her hands to her sides.

Denver spoke up quickly. "You're right about that, Judge McCray. I wish I'd thought to bring gloves with me, but somehow when I was packing for a trip south, it never occurred to me."

The judge laughed. "I can understand that, but you just keep in mind that in Barbourville, you have to be prepared for changes in the weather. As we like to say around these parts, 'If you don't like the weather, stick around. It'll change soon.' Now let's go eat. My dear Evelyn is giving me one of those looks that means I'd better mind my manners." He laughed again while gently herding Mattie and Denver toward their places.

Conversation around the table involved small talk about the weather until everyone had been served. Then talk shifted to the news in town.

Eloise looked toward Denver. "I had hoped your brother might join us today, but he and Richard were called out of town unexpectedly this morning. They left for Atlanta around ten thirty, something about the financing for their new venture. But I'm sure Dallas has told you all about that."

Denver laid his sandwich on his plate. "He mentioned something to me a few days ago. He and Richard have bought a tract of land in the county and are planning a development, right?"

"Yes, Richard's quite excited about it. The tract lies along the top of a bluff and has a fantastic view. He and Dallas have already hired a landscape architect to help ensure that all of the land's unique features are kept intact when they actually start construction."

The judge turned toward Mattie. "Perhaps this plan for a new development is something you'll want to include in your article, Miz Meadows."

His wife spoke up immediately. "No, no, Bob. Miss Meadows is more interested in the historical aspects of town, isn't that right, my dear?"

Everyone looked at Mattie, who felt blood rushing to her face. She didn't really require information about either the past or the future of the town in order to write her article about the cottage, but she didn't want to say so. Fortunately she was saved from answering when Lily Martin interjected an apology.

"My assistant called me on my cell phone and told me you'd stopped by the library this morning, Mattie. I'm sorry I missed you again. If you wish, we can make an appointment so I'll be sure to be there when you come back."

Mattie looked toward the woman she had earlier suspected of being her mother and suppressed a sigh. She felt no sense of kinship with Lily Martin, but she had recently become convinced she wouldn't recognize her mother if she saw her. It was essential, she realized, that she keep an open mind.

"Yes, I'd love to make an appointment with you. I'm hoping you can point me to some interesting reading materials about the county's history."

The librarian raised her brows. "I feel sure my assistant could have been as useful to you as I, but I'll be happy to meet with you. Unfortunately, there isn't a lot of local history located in the library." She looked at their hostess. "Evelyn probably has a better collection of county memorabilia than we do."

Mattie glanced toward Evelyn, who smiled and nodded. "I suspected that Lily might steer you in my direction, my dear, so I've already made copies of the articles I've written over the years about our town's history. I wrote the articles because I once envisioned having a column in the local newspaper, but I eventually realized that I didn't have time to be consistent about it so I gave up on that idea. I'll give you a folder when you leave, and you can peruse my articles at your leisure."

"I appreciate that very much," Mattie said before turning to the librarian. "So it looks as though it won't be necessary for us to set up an appointment after all, although I appreciate your willingness to meet with me."

The librarian smiled and nodded. "Just give me a call if you change your mind."

Eloise pushed back from the table. "This has been wonderful, as always, Bob and Evelyn, but I have a client coming this afternoon and I need to prepare for our meeting, so I'll have to run. Thank you so much for inviting me."

Mattie glanced at Denver, who nodded. "We'd better go, too," Mattie said.

Evelyn smiled and stood. "It's been so lovely having everyone here. Mattie, the articles I mentioned are in a folder that is lying on the table in the entrance hall. Don't let me forget to give it to you."

The judge also got to his feet, and Mattie watched him closely. The man was rumored to be exceptionally intelligent, and she was beginning to wonder if perhaps he suspected her of ulterior motives in hanging around town so long.

She looked on as his gaze cut to his wife and a wistful

smile touched his lips. His expression softened, and for a split second, Mattie imagined that moisture had brightened his eyes. Then his gaze shifted and locked with Mattie's. His eyes narrowed for a split second before he affected his usual jovial grin. "Well now, Miz Meadows, I'm real happy you could join us today. You'll have to come back again before you leave town, you hear?"

Mattie murmured an agreement before expressing her appreciation for lunch. She then turned to Denver, who fell in step beside her as they moved toward the front of the house.

Ten minutes later, with Miss Evelyn's folder grasped firmly in her hand, Mattie climbed into the passenger's seat of Denver's car, heaved a deep sigh of relief, and leaned back against the soft upholstery. She couldn't wait to get back to the cottage so she and Denver could share a pot of coffee and their impressions about all that had happened to them in Barbourville that day.

Ten

Denver took his eye off the road long enough to glance at the folder Evelyn McCray had given Mattie as they left the farmhouse after lunch. Mattie had been flipping through the contents while he drove back toward the cottage. "Anything interesting in there?" he asked.

She sighed. "Not so far, at least not for my purposes. But then I didn't really expect much so I'm not disappointed."

Denver flipped on his signal before turning left onto Potter Street. He hoped Mattie didn't plan to go back to the B and B just yet. "Want to join me at the cottage for a cup of coffee?"

She shot him a smile. "I was hoping you'd ask. I'd like your feedback about what happened at the judge's house today."

"Sure thing." Denver rolled to a stop in front of the cottage. "I'm not sure how much help I can be, but I'm available to listen."

Dealing with Denver

Half an hour later, Denver sat across from Mattie at the kitchen table, coffee cup in hand, and admitted that he really couldn't confirm her suspicion that Eloise and Judge McCray had noticed her symptoms of Raynaud's Disease.

"It's possible they noticed," he said. "But personally I wasn't aware that your fingers had turned white. I figured out what was going on while you were holding your hands up to the fire, but that was mainly because I could tell from your expression that something was wrong."

Mattie blew out her breath in a long sigh. "Maybe I'm just being paranoid. Maybe neither of them paid any attention to my hands at all."

Denver picked up the carafe and topped off their coffee before meeting Mattie's gaze. "You know you're just spinning your wheels here, don't you?"

She raised her brows. "You still think I should talk to the sheriff, don't you?"

"Look, Mattie. I know Daniel. He's a good man, and he would never allow loyalty to his family to take precedence over his responsibilities as sheriff."

"I believe you, Denver, but I'd hate to put Daniel in that position if I can avoid it. If someone in his family is really trying to keep my existence a secret, that person probably wouldn't appreciate Daniel's interference. Besides, my desire to find my mother doesn't really fall under Daniel's responsibilities as sheriff."

"I don't think Daniel would see it that way, but the decision is up to you."

Mattie sighed again, then started massaging her forehead with her fingertips. "Darn it. I seemed to have worried myself right into a fierce headache. I do that sometimes. I think I'll go back to the B and B and take a nap."

Denver pushed his coffee cup away. "Do you have something to take for your headache?"

"Yes. But I've discovered that sleep is the best medicine. I usually sleep for several hours."

"Why don't you call me when you wake up? If you're feeling better and are interested, we can get some dinner together."

Mattie pushed back from the table and stood. "I'll call but don't wait dinner on me."

"Do you feel like driving? I'll be glad to take you to the B and B and pick you up later."

Mattie gifted him with a weak smile. "Thanks, Denver, but I'll be fine."

"You're sure?"

Mattie nodded, then flinched. "Positive. I'll be okay as soon as I take something and lie down a while. I'll call you later."

Denver would have preferred driving her but he didn't want to delay her by arguing so he settled for walking her to her car and watching until she turned the corner and drove out of sight.

Now at loose ends, he wandered over to Dallas' house where he passed the time by playing with his nephew until Beth Ann announced it was time for Matthew's nap. By that time, Beth Ann had started cooking dinner and invited Denver to stay.

He hesitated for only a couple of seconds. After all, Beth Ann was a great cook, and besides, he didn't want to face eating at the cottage alone. He figured if Mattie wanted to find him, she'd know where to look.

Half an hour later, Dallas came through the back door. He looked harried and tired, but he smiled when he saw Denver seated at the kitchen table helping Beth Ann put a salad together.

"Just the fellow I wanted to see." Dallas slipped off his jacket and hung it over the back of a chair.

Denver glanced over his shoulder to see if someone else had entered the room unbeknownst to him. He wasn't accustomed to Dallas greeting him with such camaraderie. When he realized he was the object of his brother's enthusiasm, he narrowed his eyes. "Okay, Dallas, what do you want?"

Dallas pulled out a chair and sat down at the table across from Beth Ann. He shot her a quick smile and wink. "I could sure use a cup of coffee. It's still darn cold outside."

Beth Ann finished slicing a radish and laid her knife on the table. "I'll get you some coffee. Fortunately I brewed a pot of decaf for supper. But first, where have you been all of this time and why didn't you call?"

Dallas winced. "I forgot to take my cell phone, and Richard doesn't even own one, if you can believe that."

A few seconds later Beth Ann set a cup of coffee on the

table in front of Dallas, then shot him a frown. "And they've removed all of the landlines between here and Atlanta, have they?"

Dallas winced again. "I'm sorry, sweetheart. The thing is, we were unbelievably busy. The investment company is breathing down our necks, wanting us to get started while it's still spring in hopes we'll have some of the units ready before winter."

Beth Ann relented, smiled, and bent to give Dallas a quick kiss. "So what's the hold-up?"

Dallas glanced at Denver. "We need an expert in electronics."

Denver glanced up from the cucumber he was paring. "Don't look at me, brother. I have a tiny bit of expertise in a tiny corner of the electronics universe. That's it. You need someone who has their own business."

"You could start your own business."

"Are you insane? I'm an attorney, not a businessman."

"Face it, Denver. You only went into law because Dayton and I were going into law and you were in the habit of sticking close to us to keep us in line. Your true love was always anything to do with mechanics and, more recently, electronics. That's why you spend so much of your free time helping Steve."

"Even if that's true, I've spent years building a career as an attorney."

"True, but I was an attorney myself until I decided to

go into renovations. Now I'm going into construction. You could go into security and electronics. Home buyers today are looking for all the bells and whistles. Wi-fi, of course, but that's just a beginning. They want the latest in security systems plus built-in entertainment systems. I know you've helped Steve with that type of installation."

"Helped is the operative word there, Dallas. I helped him. He did all the buying, all the planning, all the everything. I just got out of bed on an occasional Saturday morning and helped him."

"Steve would help you now if you asked him. He'd tell you everything you needed to know to get started in your own business."

Denver shook his head. "I can't believe you're even suggesting such a thing."

"Why not? I can tell that you like Barbourville. And you seemed to love the old Masterson place out on highway one-fifty-two."

"Was that the old stone house with that big front porch?"

"Yep."

"I mentioned that to Mattie. She'd like to see it too. Can you make arrangements for us to tour the house?"

"Sure. I can even make arrangements for you to buy the house. You could live there. You and Mattie."

"Whoa!" Denver glared at his brother. "You're moving a bit fast here, numbskull. I like Mattie but we just met a couple of days ago."

Dallas merely smiled. "I know, but sometimes meeting is all that's required. I knew the first time I saw Beth Ann that she was the girl for me."

He ignored Beth Ann's soft snort coming from somewhere in the vicinity of the kitchen stove. "And I think Mattie likes you in return."

Denver punched his brother on the shoulder. "Will you stop it? I'm not going into business so you'll have someone to help keep the investors off your back. You got yourself into this, and you can get yourself out."

Beth Ann dropped into a chair and grasped Dallas' hand. "Are they really bugging you, sweetheart?"

Dallas shrugged. "Nothing Richard and I can't handle. But you know Richard. He's determined this development is going to be the best planned ever, and we really are having trouble finding someone willing to invest their time in doing the security and the electronics the way it should be done. Most businesses we've approached just want to slap together a package that doesn't take into account the needs of individual homeowners. The smaller units that we're building for the older homeowners don't need the same level of sophisticated electronics that the units built for growing families will require."

Denver frowned. "What's this? I thought you were just building big, beautiful houses for executives from the surrounding cities to use as summer homes."

"Not at all. We're building a community where career

people can live with their growing families. But there'll be smaller bungalows scattered about in case those career people want to bring their aging parents along."

Beth Ann chimed in. "Right. Or in case a young family can only afford a small place to start with. There'll be a shopping area and a clubhouse and hopefully all the necessities within walking distance of most of the houses."

"That sounds appealing. I wonder..." Denver paused to stare into space.

Dallas waited a minute, then tapped his foot a few seconds. "What? I can tell your brain is slowly grinding away, struggling to string one thought after another. How about sharing a clue with us?"

"How about shutting your big yap for a minute so I can think?"

Dallas glanced at Beth Ann, grinned unrepentantly, and took a sip of his coffee. A minute passed in silence before Denver finally spoke up.

"You're thinking really high tech? Say along the lines of computer-controlled electronics that could be handled from a central panel?"

"For the most sophisticated houses, sure."

"Where people could touch a button in the kitchen to light their fireplace in the den?"

"Yes!" Dallas' tone grew increasingly enthusiastic. "Or they could control the level of lighting in the den, turn on a CD player in the bedroom, that type of thing."

"Steve's done some of that type of work in a few houses, mostly for friends or family members, but I know he enjoyed it. And he's been talking about expanding. He might be interested in going into a partnership with me. I could talk to him about it."

Dallas' eyes brightened. "That would be great. I know Steve has one of the most highly regarded security businesses in Chicago, but I didn't know he has that kind of experience with advanced electronics. Do you think he'd be interested in adding that facet to his business?"

"I don't know but I can ask him."

"Great! When?"

"I'll call him tonight and float the idea. Knowing Steve, he'll want some time to think about it, but I'd say he'll be very interested."

Dallas' expression grew solemn. "You realize, don't you, that if you and Steve go into business together in Tennessee, you'll need to move here?"

Denver lifted his shoulders in a slight shrug. "I'll have to think about that too. I'll need a week or so before I can give you a definite answer."

"I can wait a week or two if there's a possibility the answer might be affirmative."

Beth Ann stood. "Dinner should be ready to put on the table, guys, if you're ready to eat."

"I'm ready," Denver said. What he didn't say, because he certainly didn't know the answer yet, was whether he was ready to give up his cozy niche in Chicago for the uncertainties of a new business in a different part of the country. And to be honest with himself, Denver realized that part of the current allure of Barbourville revolved around Mattie's presence here. Just thinking about her brought a smile of pleasure to his face.

But Barbourville wasn't Mattie's home, and even if she managed to locate her mother here, there was a strong possibility the reunion would not be a happy one. Either way, chances were good that Mattie would not want to hang around Barbourville more than a couple more days.

In that case, Denver wasn't sure he'd be happy moving from Chicago to this tiny town, even to help out his brother. He decided to talk to Steve before he gave the matter any more thought. Maybe Steve would have some ideas about how they could work out a partnership. Or even if they should try.

Denver didn't get back to the cottage until almost nine o'clock, and while he wanted to call Mattie, he didn't want to disturb her if she was still sleeping off her headache.

He glanced at his watch, realized it was only eight o'clock in Chicago, and promptly dialed Steve's home phone number.

Half an hour later when Denver hung up the phone, he had talked Steve into coming to Barbourville the following week to look around in consideration of opening a branch of his business in Tennessee. He was still sitting beside the phone when it rang.

As he had hoped, Mattie was on the other end. "Hi," she said. "What are you doing?"

"I just hung up from talking to my friend Steve."

A note of worry crept into Mattie's voice. "I hope nothing's wrong in Chicago."

"No, nothing like that. Just business. How's your headache?"

"Completely gone, thanks."

"I'm glad. Say, are you free in the morning? I was hoping you'd go with me to inspect the Masterson place. Dallas loaned me the key so we could get in."

Mattie hesitated. "I'm not sure. I need to talk to you about something. Could I come by for a few minutes in the morning?"

"Sure. What time?"

"Around nine o'clock if that's okay with you."

"Fine. Have you had dinner?"

"No. I slept most of the afternoon after taking my headache medicine. What about you?"

Denver straightened in his chair. "I had dinner but I could use a cup of decaf. Why don't I pick you up? We can drive over to Smithwood and you can get something to eat at the coffee shop over there."

"Will it be open this late?"

"It should be. Remember when I picked up the ingredients for the buttermilk pies?"

"Yes."

"Since it was a Sunday, I had to drive to Smithwood to

the grocery store, and while I was there, I stopped by the coffee shop to check it out. Their sign said they're open until midnight every night."

"Okay then. I'll wait for you downstairs."

"I'll see you in twenty minutes."

* * *

Half an hour later when Mattie settled into the passenger seat of Denver's car, she felt the tension draining from her back and shoulders for the first time all day. Being with Denver, she had discovered, was an enthralling combination of excitement and tranquility. She'd never felt this way before, and she wasn't sure what to think of the sensation.

On the other hand, she had no difficulty at all in identifying the sensation she felt when he reached across the front seat to grasp her hand, then leaned toward her. Warmth moved up her arm. Even without thinking, she leaned toward him.

Their kiss was brief, just lips touching lips in a short and sizzling instant, but it was enough. Mattie had suspected she was falling in love with Denver Vance. Tonight she was sure. She hadn't planned to fall in love. She certainly hadn't wanted to fall in love.

But her relationship with Denver felt very much like falling in love. When the slightest touch could send her emotions swirling like a leaf caught in the vortex of a Dogwood winter wind, she knew she was falling in love.

Denver smiled at her, winked, and turned the key in the ignition. The Mercedes started with a quiet purr that masked the power of the engine, much, Mattie reflected, as Denver's laid-back personality masked the strength that resided beneath his serenity. She'd never known a man who was so steady, so calming, so ready to stand beside her and support her when she needed his strength. On the other hand, he appeared to totally respect her independence.

He pulled out onto the highway leading through the countryside toward Smithwood. "Do you want to talk yet?"

Mattie looked at him. His eyes were on the road ahead, but a muscle jumped in his jaw and she became aware that he was much less sanguine than he appeared. She had been keeping him in suspense, she realized, but he hadn't complained. She decided to speak up immediately.

"I've decided I want to follow your advice and go to the sheriff. I'm getting nowhere on my own, and I'm hoping that after breakfast in the morning, you'll go with me to talk to Daniel."

Denver glanced at her. His expression gave no clue as to what he was thinking. "Are you going to tell him that you suspect one of his uncles might have been involved with your adoption?"

"Yes, I plan to tell him all I know and all I suspect. I had hoped, as you are well aware, to discover something on my own, but that apparently isn't going to happen."

Denver nodded. "I think you're doing the right thing."

"You'll come with me then?"

"Of course. Do you want to go right after breakfast?"

"If that's all right with you. We could go to the Masterson place after our visit with Daniel if you're still interested."

The muscle in Denver's jaw jumped again. "I think I might be, yes."

Mattie watched him closely. "Why are you so interested in the Masterson place if you're going back to Chicago in a few days?"

Denver's lips thinned and he had opened his mouth to speak just as the lights of Smithwood came into view. He sighed, then appeared to relax. "Why don't I explain while you have dinner?"

Mattie looked out the windshield as Denver turned into the parking lot of a small building. "That sounds good. I'm famished."

"Haven't you had anything to eat since lunch?"

She shook her head. "No, and frankly, I was a little too nervous to eat much at the McCray's house."

"No wonder you're hungry. As I recall, this coffee shop has a good selection of soups and sandwiches."

Once inside, Mattie ordered a bowl of vegetable soup and a BLT while Denver settled for a cup of coffee.

"Sure you don't want a piece of pie?" Mattie asked when her meal was served.

"I'd better not. Beth Ann had blackberry cobbler and vanilla ice cream for dessert tonight. I'm still stuffed."

Mattie sipped a spoonful of her soup. "And I'm jealous that you got to eat dinner with Beth Ann and Dallas. Your sister-in-law is a wonderful cook. But you were going to tell me something about your interest in the Masterson place."

Denver wrapped his hand around the coffee mug. "I talked to Steve tonight."

"Yes, you mentioned that earlier." Mattie bit into her sandwich but continued to watch Denver.

"He and I might be going into a partnership. Here in Barbourville. Dallas wants us to provide the security and electronics work for the development he and Richard have started."

Mattie laid her sandwich in her plate. "Oh, wow! That's quite a departure from what you've been doing. Does the idea really appeal to you?"

"Yeah it does. I've always loved tinkering with mechanical things. When my brothers and I still lived at home, I was the one who kept the lawn mower running in the summer or figured out why Dad's car wouldn't start on cold mornings in the winter. Everybody counted on me to keep our electrical appliances running, and I enjoyed doing it."

Mattie thought about his statement for a minute, then frowned. "But would there be enough business in Barbourville to support a business over the long haul?"

"Initially, yes, because Dallas' and Richard's development is going to be a big one. After that, there'd probably be some traveling involved. We might have to spread out as far east as Knoxville or south to Chattanooga. We could even do work in Atlanta if we had to."

Mattie took a sip of her coffee. "I can see that you've given this quite a bit of thought."

Denver nodded. "But going into business with Steve isn't my only reason for wanting to move."

Mattie gulped, then picked up her sandwich and took a huge bite. She wasn't sure she was ready to talk about the future yet. There were simply too many unknowns in her present.

Denver sighed. "Aren't you going to ask me what else interests me in this part of the country?"

Chewing vigorously, Mattie pointed to her bulging cheeks and shook her head.

Denver shrugged. "I get it. You don't want to talk about that right now. Okay. No problem. But I'm really glad you've decided to talk to the sheriff. If anyone can and will help you, it's Daniel."

Mattie swallowed and reached across the table to grasp Denver's hand. She appreciated him so much. He was behaving just as she had expected him to—with understanding and a willingness to give her the space she needed to try to discover who she was and what her future would hold, either with him or alone.

But suddenly a future without Denver held no appeal at all. If she was to be honest with herself, she had to admit that the thought of staying in Barbourville with Denver, the two of them building a life together, was just about the most wonderful future she could envision.

On the other hand, that perfect future could deteriorate into a morass of illness and heartbreak if her Raynaud's Disease was not genetic but instead was an early symptom of an insidious disease that would gradually infiltrate their lives and finally, perhaps, put an end to hers.

She couldn't take a chance on the latter scenario being the one that became their reality. She had to know one way or the other before she could make a commitment of any sort to Denver.

She still held his hand in hers. She tightened her grasp and forced a smile. "You'll come with me to see the sheriff tomorrow morning, won't you?"

Denver didn't return her smile but he held her gaze. "You know I will."

"In that case…" Mattie released his hand and pushed back from the table. "In that case, I'd better get back to the B and B. I'd like to get an early start tomorrow morning. If Daniel is willing to help me, then perhaps you and I will still have time to check out the Masterson place."

Denver's smile was both sad and relieved. "I'll hold you to that tomorrow, because I know Daniel well enough to be sure he'll help you."

"Even if the knowledge might discomfort someone in his family?"

"Even then."

"Okay." Mattie stood. "I'll plan on coming by the cottage and picking you up around eight thirty if that's okay with you."

Denver also stood. "Fine with me," he said. "In fact, I'll be looking forward to it."

Eleven

Denver contented himself with a quick if passionate kiss when he walked Mattie to the door of the B and B. He would have liked to linger, but the expression in her eyes told him quite clearly that her emotional state was fragile. He could only hope that after they saw Daniel the following morning, she would feel a bit more at peace.

By the time he had driven back to the cottage, it was almost one o'clock in the morning, but he knew he wouldn't be able to sleep for a while. He went to the kitchen, fixed himself a cup of decaf, and settled down at the table to think.

He knew, even without Mattie telling him, that their future depended on what she could find out about her parentage. He would never be able to convince Mattie that if she failed to find her mother, he cared for her enough to deal with whatever challenges the future might hold for the two of them.

And he certainly wasn't going to give up without a fight. Even if she didn't find her mother in Barbourville, they could keep looking.

But based on what Mattie had discovered thus far, Denver had a strong suspicion that her birth mother did, in fact, have some connection to the McCray family. And he fully believed that Daniel would do all in his power to help Mattie find that connection.

That knowledge finally gave Denver the peace of mind he needed in order to go to bed and get some sleep.

When his alarm went off at seven o'clock the next morning, he climbed out of bed, eager to start the day. He and Mattie would visit Daniel, lay her suspicions about her mother at his feet, and then drive out to the Masterson place.

He could hardly wait to show Mattie around the house that had appealed to him from the first moment he'd laid eyes on it. For reasons Denver couldn't begin to understand, the old Masterson place had immediately felt like home to him although it was nothing like the house he owned in Chicago.

It was larger, for one thing, which was fortunate. The original house had been built in the early 1900s and had featured large rooms but only a couple of closets and no bathrooms. Ill-planned modernizations over the years had chopped up the large rooms into smaller, unattractive areas. When Dallas bought the house, he had gutted it and reclaimed the early charm while adding features that were now considered necessities, like large bathrooms and plenty of storage space. Denver wanted to own that house. But only if Mattie also loved it and would consider someday sharing it with him.

An hour later, Denver carried a cup of coffee out onto the front porch to wait for Mattie. Dogwood winter had come and gone. The sun was already warming the air, and the cheerful call of birds nesting in the maples combined with the fragrance of clean air to banish memories of the recent cold spell.

Cradling his coffee, Denver stood near the edge of the porch, enjoying the sounds of the neighbors starting their activities for another day. Car doors slammed as parents either prepared to leave for work or buckled up their children for the drive to school.

A smile brightened Denver's face when he looked toward the corner and saw Mattie's car turning onto Potter Street. His smile quickly faded when he realized she was driving just a bit too fast. When she skidded to a stop with one tire on the sidewalk and flung her car door open, he slammed his coffee cup down on a porch post and dashed down the steps to meet her.

She jumped out and ran around the front of the car and into Denver's arms. Her entire body trembled. He pulled her close, holding her tightly. He felt her heart pounding, and his own sped up as fear for her pushed adrenaline into his system.

"Mattie? What's wrong? Can you tell me what's upset you so?"

She pulled back a bit and turned her head to look down the street first one way and then the other. "Can we go inside?" she asked, her voice shaky.

Half expecting someone to be chasing her, Denver also looked up and down the street. There wasn't a car or a human in sight. "Sure we can go inside." He released her, then quickly wrapped an arm around her waist. "Let's go."

Mattie's trembling had subsided by the time they reached the front porch. Seconds later when they stepped into the cottage's entrance hall, she heaved a sigh. "I'm sorry, Denver. I probably overreacted. Can we go to the kitchen and sit down a minute?"

"Of course." Denver grasped her hand and they walked together to the kitchen. When Mattie dropped into a chair at the table, Denver grabbed a clean cup out of the cabinet and poured her some coffee, then retrieved one of her flavored creams out of the refrigerator.

She rewarded him with a tremulous smile before doctoring her coffee. Denver didn't bother with a cup for himself. Instead he sat down, rested his elbows on the table, and regarded Mattie with a slight frown. "You want to tell me what's upset you so much?"

She nodded, then ran her hand into the pocket of her jacket and pulled out a folded piece of paper. "I found this under my windshield wiper this morning." She handed it across the table to him.

Denver unfolded the paper and read aloud. "We know why you're here. Your presence is a danger to the peace of mind of a wonderful woman, and she doesn't deserve having her life disrupted by you. Please go away and leave us alone."

He looked across the table and into Mattie's tear-filled eyes. She tried for a smile, but it was weak. "At least I know my mother's here somewhere," she said.

Denver clenched his teeth. It would do Mattie no good for him to express his fury at the person who'd written that unsigned note. "We can take this with us to the sheriff's office," he said. "It's proof that you were right to come looking for your mother here in McCray County."

"I'm not going to see the sheriff," Mattie said. She blinked away the tears and lifted her coffee cup to her lips. She set it back down without taking a sip. "I'm leaving town this morning."

Denver had feared this would be her reaction. He doubted he could change her mind, but he had to try. "You don't know who wrote that note, but it indicates to me that your mother doesn't know you're in town. Perhaps she wouldn't want you to go without contacting her. At least show the note to the sheriff and give him a chance to investigate."

"Oh, but I do know who wrote the note," Mattie said. Her eyes filled with tears again. "Don't you recognize the paper?"

Denver looked at the note again. The top edge of the sheet was uneven, as though it had been hastily trimmed with a pair of scissors. The paper itself was cream-colored and heavier than most. "Eloise," he said, recalling the map she'd drawn for them the day before.

Mattie nodded. "I doubt anyone else in town has stationery printed on that quality of vellum. And you'll notice that her name has been trimmed off of the top."

"Do you think she's your mother?"

"I don't know, but if she is, she obviously doesn't want anything to do with me."

"Personally, I think we should go directly to her office right now, this morning. You can explain why you want to find your mother. Surely she'd understand if you explain that for your peace of mind, you really need to know the source of your Raynaud's Disease."

"That's just it." Mattie lifted her chin. "There's no longer any reason for me to track down my mother. I've already learned that my Raynaud's Disease is genetic."

Denver frowned. "What do you mean?"

"I'm positive the judge and Eloise noticed that my fingers had turned white during the cold snap yesterday. Then I received the note today. Obviously they recognized my condition and they know someone else who experiences the same symptoms, which led them to guess my parentage."

"At least that's good news," Denver said. "You don't have to worry anymore that your Raynaud's is an early symptom of something much worse."

"True." Mattie sighed. "I suppose I should feel happier than I do. I guess I didn't really understand until now just how much I'd counted on at least identifying my mother. I'd honestly convinced myself it was all about the medical condition, but now I realize it was much more. I'd hoped to find my mother and maybe connect in some way. Obviously that's not going to happen."

"That's her loss," Denver said, his tone laced with anger. "Whoever she is, she should be proud to have such a talented and wonderful daughter."

"Thank you." Mattie smiled, then lifted her shoulders in a slight shrug. "Guess she doesn't see it that way." She pushed her chair back and stood. "I've got to go now, Denver."

He stood too. "Where? Where are you going?"

"Right now, back to the B and B to finish packing. Then home, to my apartment in Georgia. I wish things could have been different for us, but we have to be practical. We each have our own lives and our own careers. It only makes sense to go our separate ways. Thanks for everything you've done for me."

Tears filled her eyes again and she turned and hurried toward the front of the cottage. Denver caught up with her just as she pulled the front door open. He put a hand on her shoulder and gently turned her to face him.

"Don't go, Mattie," he said softly. "What we feel for each other is too wonderful to abandon without giving it a fighting chance. Stay another day at least. Come with me to visit the Masterson place. We could settle right here, in

Barbourville, between Chicago and Georgia, and create a future together."

Mattie shook her head. "I couldn't live in Barbourville, Denver, not when I know my mother lives here and doesn't want to acknowledge me."

Denver wasn't willing to give up easily. "I think too much of you to let you walk out of my life, Matilda Meadows. You and I could build a future together anywhere in this country. It doesn't have to be in Barbourville."

"I won't have you giving up all you're about to establish here, Denver. You've talked to Steve about starting a new business here. You've found a house you like here in the county with your brother and niece. Don't talk about giving it up and moving somewhere different for me. I won't let you."

She started to turn but paused when Denver grabbed her hand.

"I know you're upset," he said. "And you have every right to be upset. But Mattie, you don't have to let your mother's rejection of you destroy our future together."

Mattie shook her head. The tears she'd managed to hold back all morning now swelled and spilled over, tracing warm tracks down her cheeks. She shook her head again.

"You don't understand, Denver. I can't live here, knowing my mother is in this town but not knowing who she is. Every time I walked down the sidewalk, I'd be trying to guess if the woman meeting me was my mother. Anytime I went to a dinner party, I'd wonder if she might be sitting at the same table with me but refusing to acknowledge me as her daughter. I couldn't handle that, Denver. I'm so sorry, but I just couldn't."

She jerked free of his grasp and turned back toward the porch, only to come face to face with Evelyn McCray, who regarded her with widened eyes.

Aware that she'd almost slammed into the sweet lady who'd shared information about the county's history with her, Mattie gasped and stepped backward, stopping only when she backed into Denver's chest. "Oh! Miss Evelyn. I'm so sorry. I didn't know you were there."

Evelyn McCray stared at Mattie for a few seconds, then slowly shook her head. "How could you know I was behind you today, my dear? I was never there for you at any time in the past, now was I?"

TWELVE

As the probable meaning of Evelyn McCray's words sank in, Mattie's world slowly tilted. Her head began to swim, and she supposed she must have slumped because Denver immediately reached to grasp her shoulders, offering his unwavering support. Mattie opened her mouth and forced words out through lips that had gone numb. "What are you talking about, Miss Evelyn? Surely you can't mean that you...?"

Tears swelled in the older woman's eyes and her rosy cheeks slowly paled. "That I'm your mother? Yes, that's exactly what I mean. And if you choose to hate me for the rest of your life, I'll understand. Just please be aware that I didn't know who you were when you first came to town and I only began to suspect a couple of days ago that you were my daughter. I knew for sure yesterday when I saw your fingers turning white just as mine do when the weather becomes chilly."

"Oh my." Mattie continued to stare at the judge's wife through widened eyes. Never would she have guessed that this sweet little lady was her mother. Evelyn McCray seemed so genteel, so unassuming, it was impossible for Mattie to imagine her giving birth to a child and then giving that child away.

At a loss for words, Mattie breathed a silent sigh of relief when Denver spoke up. "Miss Evelyn, please come in and join me and Mattie for a cup of coffee. I imagine you would like to visit with your daughter for a while."

Evelyn nodded. "I would. If Mattie's willing."

Still speechless, Mattie stepped back into the entrance hall, making way for Evelyn to come inside. Denver was there, of course, waiting to support her in whatever she chose to do. She had no doubt that he would have asked Evelyn to leave if Mattie had indicated that was her wish.

Finally she found her voice. "Yes, please, Miss Evelyn. I'd like for you to stay a while and talk if you will."

A smile finally touched the older woman's lips and a bit of color returned to her cheeks. "Nothing in the world would make me happier, my dear."

The loud screeching of tires drew all of their attention to the street in front of the house. Eloise Smithfield's SUV skidded to a stop and Judge McCray jumped out of the passenger's side. Eloise herself stepped out more slowly on the driver's side.

"Oh dear," Evelyn murmured. "My misguided protectors have arrived."

The judge hurried across the grass and bounded up the steps to the front porch. He paused in the doorway and glared at Mattie. "What are you saying to my wife?" he demanded.

"Stop it, Bob," Evelyn said, her tone firm. Color flooded her cheeks. "You don't know what you're talking about or who you're talking to."

"And you do?"

"Of course." Evelyn looked past her husband. Eloise had just stepped up behind him. "Why are you chauffeuring Bob around this morning, Eloise?"

Denver stepped forward. "Why don't you all come into the living room and sit down? Obviously there are questions on everyone's mind. We might as well try to find some answers."

Mattie reached for Denver's hand. "Thanks, Denver. That's a wonderful idea." She also grasped Evelyn's hand. "Shall we?"

"Absolutely, my dear." Evelyn squared her shoulders and addressed her husband and Eloise. "You might as well come inside and hear this too. Everyone in town is going to know soon enough."

The judge pushed his way into the entrance hall and to his wife's side. "Now my dear, there's no reason for you to feel—"

"Hush Bob," Evelyn interrupted. "There's every reason for me to admit to what I did all those years ago—at least to you and Mattie. You two are more intimately involved than anyone else. But let's sit down and talk like civilized people. There's no need for your gruffness today."

Evelyn nodded to Denver. "Lead the way, please, Mr. Vance. I'm very appreciative of your kindness."

Five minutes later everyone had taken a seat in the cottage's small living room. Denver and Mattie sat side by side on the loveseat. Although they weren't touching, his arm rested on the back of the seat only inches from her shoulders. The judge had tugged on his wife's hand until she dropped down beside him on the sofa. He then intertwined his fingers with hers and held on tightly.

Eloise selected a straight chair near the doorway to the entrance hall. She hadn't said a word since arriving on the scene, but she was the first to speak after everyone was seated. "I owe you an apology, Miss Meadows. I thought I was protecting a friend."

A frown furrowed Evelyn's brow. "What did you do, Eloise?"

Color burned high on Eloise's cheeks. "I wrote Miss Meadows a note telling her to get out of town."

"My goodness! Why would you…? Oh, of course! Richard must have told you that I'd had a baby and given it up for adoption."

"He didn't knowingly tell me, but I've known since the beginning. I was sitting in a booth at the Student Union and overheard him and Josh making plans with that classmate of Josh's to help you make arrangements to give your baby up for adoption."

Evelyn turned to her husband. "And you knew all these years, too, Bob?"

He nodded. "Also by accident, shortly before our wedding. Josh and Richard had joined us for the rehearsal dinner. Afterwards, they'd gone out into the parking lot and I decided to join them. They were standing beside Josh's car, and neither saw me approaching. They were speculating as to whether you'd tell me that you'd given birth to a baby girl and given her up for adoption. I purposely started shuffling my feet so they'd know I was in the vicinity, and they shut up immediately."

Tears welled in Evelyn's eyes. "You could have called off the wedding," she said.

"And give up an opportunity to marry the most wonderful girl in the world? I wasn't that much of a fool, my dear. Although I always wished you had trusted me enough to confide in me."

The tears in Evelyn's eyes spilled over. "It was never from a lack of trust in you, Bob. But I'd promised Mattie's father that I'd give her up for adoption and never tell anyone about her birth."

Mattie's eyes widened in horror. "What kind of man would ask that of you?"

"The kind who was dying and who knew his family would try to take custody of you if they'd known you existed. They would have succeeded, too, and he didn't want his child subjected to life with his family."

Eloise lifted both hands to cradle her face. "Oh my goodness," she murmured. "You had Tommy Kessler's baby."

"Evelyn?" the judge asked, staring at her with widened eyes.

Evelyn looked into her husband's eyes and nodded. "You know that Tommy and I went to college in the same town. Mine was a church school and Tommy's was that exclusive private institution.

"But Tommy was miserable there. He'd never been comfortable with the social and political ambitions his family possessed, and the other students at his school were just as hard and unfeeling as his family. He and I started spending a lot of time together."

"Wait," Mattie said. "Tommy Kessler? As in Kessler Boulevard, the main street in Barbourville? Those Kesslers?"

"Yes," Evelyn said. "Those Kesslers. They were one of the founding families of Barbourville. Tommy was their younger son. The older one, Marshall, had just one daughter before he crashed his private plane into the side of a mountain.

"After Marshall's death, the family pinned their hopes on Tommy, but he wasn't like the rest of them. He didn't want to impose his will on other people. He started hanging out with me because he felt more at ease around the people in my church school than those in his private school."

"And then you fell in love," the judge said.

Evelyn patted his hand. "We did, yes, but we kept our relationship a secret because we didn't want his family to find out. We knew they would disapprove because I was from a poor family, and we were afraid they'd take their spite out on my parents, who were still living at that time.

"Tommy had developed a cough over the winter, and we both assumed it was a lingering cold or allergies. About the time we discovered I was pregnant, his cough was diagnosed as cancer. It was already much too late to save him. That's when he asked me to promise to give the baby up for adoption. In order to give him peace in those last weeks, I gave him my word."

"And he died before the baby was born," Eloise said. "I remember you didn't come back to Barbourville for his funeral. I thought that was strange, but your mother said you were sick."

"I was. Sick with grief. And, of course, seven months pregnant. I could have gone to a regular adoption agency, but I was afraid word would somehow get back to Tommy's parents, so I called Josh. I knew he was in law school, and I hoped he could help me arrange an adoption. He did, of course. So I kept my promise to Tommy although it half killed me to do so. And I never expected to see my child again."

Mattie watched as tears ran down Evelyn's cheeks and fought to keep from breaking down herself. "When did you begin to suspect I was your daughter?"

"The night of Dallas' and Beth Ann's cookout. It occurred to me that you looked very much like my maternal grandmother, but then I convinced myself that because your buttermilk pies reminded me of Grandma, I was imagining the resemblance."

"You were upset though," the judge noted. "You spent the next day in bed."

"Yes. And then I decided I wanted to see more of Mattie, so I planned the luncheon with the intent of getting to know her better." She smiled at Mattie. "I didn't anticipate the arrival of Dogwood winter, but it worked out beautifully. When I saw your white fingers, I knew you were my daughter. It's a condition I inherited from my father. Obviously, it was passed down to you."

"As a matter of fact," Mattie said, "that's the main reason I started searching for my mother." She went on to explain her need to know whether her Raynaud's Disease was genetic or not.

"Well, my goodness," Evelyn said. "I never even knew that our condition had a name. Dad just thought it was an oddity, and so did I. Neither one of us ever asked a doctor about it because it was never a major problem for either of us."

Mattie smiled. "I suppose my being adopted made me especially curious about any physical anomaly. But let me ask you something. If the Kesslers were a founding family in Barbourville, where are they now? I haven't met anyone by that name since I've been in town."

"I can answer that," the judge said. "The family has died out with the exception of Marshall's daughter, and she sold all the Kessler property and moved away a few years ago. The last we heard of her, she was in California."

"So I won't be running into any of my father's family," Mattie noted.

"No, and it's probably just as well," Evelyn responded. "Your father was a fine man, but the other Kesslers had grown too ambitious over the years. Their lust for power had turned them into hard and uncaring people."

She turned to regard her husband. "I can't believe you've known all these years. Why didn't you say something?"

He grasped her hand and lifted it to his lips. A soft smile flickered in his eyes. "I loved you for who you were when we got married, my dear, and what had happened in your past had no effect on how I felt about you. Oh, I'll admit I never understood why you kept your motherhood a secret from me, but I assumed you had a good reason. Now that I know about your promise to Tommy, I understand completely."

Evelyn sighed and patted his hand. "Thank you, my dear." She then turned to Mattie. "I would very much like to spend more time with you if you're willing. Can you stay in town a few more days?"

"I'd like that too," Mattie said. "I can e-mail my story

about the cottage to the magazine and then stay here for at least another week if you're sure that's what you want."

"Actually, I'm hoping to introduce you as my daughter to some of our friends. Would you object to that?"

Mattie paused to think for a moment. "I'll leave that up to you. I never intended to disrupt your life, you know. I just wanted to find out about my Raynaud's Disease."

"Oh my dear, nothing could please me more than to introduce you as my daughter." She turned back to the judge. "That is, if Bob doesn't object."

The judge instantly shot Mattie a fond smile. "My dear Evelyn and I were never blessed with children, and I for one would love to acknowledge you as our daughter. In fact, Tommy Kessler was my best friend when we were boys, and I believe with all my heart that he'd be pleased to know his daughter is now a part of my family."

"I couldn't agree more, Bob," Evelyn said, addressing her husband but obviously speaking for Mattie's benefit. "Having my daughter in Barbourville with the prospect of making her known to my friends and neighbors is a dream come true for me. But we mustn't press her, Bob. Agreed?"

"What? Well, of course, my dear. Of course. If Mattie wants to take things slow, so be it. In fact, we should probably leave right now and let the girl have a few minutes alone to catch her breath."

Mattie raised no objections to the judge's suggestion. She was, in fact, feeling a bit overwhelmed, and she longed to have some time alone with Denver to get his advice on how she should proceed. She didn't really mind being acknowledged as Evelyn McCray's daughter but she wasn't sure she wanted a big production made of the fact.

Denver saw his visitors to the door and bid each of them a pleasant goodbye. When he finally managed to shut the front screen and turn back around, he walked to the doorway leading into the living room, leaned against the facing, and regarded Mattie with raised brows. "Some morning, wasn't it? Are you okay?"

Mattie nodded. "I think so. But..."

"But what?"

She stared at him with widened eyes. "Judge McCray wants to be my father."

Denver threw his head back and laughed. "I know. Better get ready for a wild ride. I overheard him telling Eloise as they were going down the front steps that he was on his way to see the mayor about using the town park for a barbecue a week from today. He wants to invite everyone in town to meet his new daughter."

Mattie moaned and dropped backward onto the loveseat. A second later she looked up, a wide grin lighting her face. "That rascal. Oh well, good thing I'm not bashful. And I'll have you by my side." She paused and her grin faded. Denver still hadn't stepped into the room. "I will have you by my side, won't I?"

Denver nodded, a solemn expression on his face. "If you want me, I'll be there," he said.

Mattie stood but didn't walk toward him. "Do you know yet what you're going to do?"

"You mean if Steve agrees to a partnership with me here in Barbourville?"

"Yes."

"I'm probably going to move to Barbourville. Dallas was right when he said a few days ago that I'd gone into law only because I felt that I needed to keep him and Dayton in line. My true love lies in all things mechanical, including, of course, electronics."

"You could stay in Chicago and work for Steve," Mattie noted.

"It wouldn't be the same as having my own business, something I could build from the ground up the way I could here in Barbourville. So my mind is made up. But what about you? You agreed to stay a week. What will you do following the judge's big barbecue?"

"First, I've got to tell my adoptive parents that I've located my birth mother. In fact, if the judge and Miss Evelyn don't object, I'll invite my entire family to the barbecue. I'd like my two families to become acquainted."

"And after that?"

Mattie took a deep breath. "I'm not sure. A lot has changed in my life in a very short period of time. It's almost more than I can take in at the moment."

Denver nodded. "You need to take some time. I can see that. But I'm hoping you'll agree that you and I need to stay in touch."

She nodded, but her expression was solemn. "I'd love to think that what you and I have found here is more than two strangers connecting in a strange place. But I need to know that our feelings won't dissipate when we're back in our own worlds. I can't see us building a future together until we're both on solid ground in the present."

Denver nodded again. "I'm sorry but not surprised that you feel that way."

She shrugged. "Your world is changing too, Denver. Not as dramatically as mine, I'll admit. You haven't just found out that you're related to half the people in Barbourville, Tennessee. But whether you agree with me or not, I'm convinced you also need some time to process what happened here between us."

Denver sighed, but he also smiled. "You make a lot of sense, Mattie Meadows. So I'll give you as much time as you need and I'll take the time you believe I should. But there's one thing you need to tell me right now. You need to tell me that I'll see you again soon."

Mattie smiled and slowly walked across the room, pausing in front of Denver, who still leaned against the door frame. She raised her right hand and cupped his cheek. "I can do that. After I get back from visiting my adoptive parents, and after the judge's barbecue is over, if you want me to, I'll go to Chicago with you. I really need to see what kind of life you're leaving behind. After that, as soon as you have time, you can visit me in Georgia and get some feel for how I grew up. How's that sound?"

"Sensible, I suppose," Denver muttered. Then his expression brightened. "As a matter of fact, I really would enjoy meeting all of your family and friends and getting to know that aspect of your personality. Not to mention the fun I'd have showing you around Chicago."

Mattie smiled. "Seeing the sights in Chicago sounds wonderful. And I'm looking forward to meeting your other brother."

Denver affected a grimace. "Okay, if you insist. Just remember that while Dayton and I may look alike, I'm the likeable one of the two."

Mattie laughed. "I'll reserve judgment on that. After all, I've seen how you and Dallas pick at each other when you're really showing affection. I suspect you and Dayton are the same."

Denver just grinned.

Mattie grinned back. "That's settled, then. In the meantime, are you still interested in showing me the old Masterson place."

Denver immediately straightened. "How soon can you be ready to go?"

Mattie moved a step closer and tilted her head back. "Just as soon as you remind me of the main reason I should be interested in seeing the old Masterson place."

Denver's grin faded while his eyes brightened and his arms slipped around Mattie's shoulders and pulled her toward him. "With pleasure," he murmured.

Their lips met, first gently, then with increasing passion. Mattie wrapped her arms around him, pulling herself closer to his chest, and was delighted to feel him deepening the kiss.

"Oh there you are." Judge McCray opened the front door and stuck his head inside the entry hall. "Glad I caught the two of you together. I wanted to invite you to a little event I have planned for a week from today."

Mattie sighed and looked past Denver's shoulder. "Okay, we'll be there."

The judge's brows shot up. "But you don't know what I'm talking about."

"The barbecue," Mattie said. "The park. The whole town invited. We'll be there. What time?"

The judge's eyes widened. "Wow, you're good. Makes me proud to be your stepdaddy. The barbecue's at eleven o'clock, rain or shine."

"Fine," Mattie said shortly. She was eager for the judge to leave so she and Denver could resume their interrupted kiss.

"Say," the judge continued, "did I just overhear you two talking about the old Masterson place?"

"Maybe," Mattie answered cautiously. "Why?"

"Oh, just that I own a nice parcel of land right next door, and if you two buy the Masterson place, why, seeing as you're my stepdaughter, I'll give you that land as a wedding present so you can expand a bit when you start raising a family. Well, bye for now. See you soon." The screen door slammed behind him.

Mattie dropped her head onto Denver's shoulder, which shook from his suppressed chuckles.

"I'm having second thoughts about someday living in McCray County," she murmured. "It's not going to be easy, having to deal with Judge McCray."

Denver smiled. "You may have to deal with me too. At least I'm hoping you'll have to deal with me too. And that you'd be willing to do so."

Mattie smiled back. "It would be a pleasure to deal with you. It's all those McCrays I worry about. After all, the county is named after them."

Denver laughed and pulled her back into his arms. "You don't have a thing to worry about, my dear. You've got Kessler blood running through your veins, and the Kessler family goes back every bit as far as the McCrays."

Mattie's eyes widened. "I hadn't thought about that." She heaved a sigh. "Okay, Mr. Vance. I suspect I'll be up for the challenge if you are."

"I definitely will be. But in the meantime, let's get back to what we were doing before the judge interrupted us."

"Great idea," Mattie said, wrapping her arms around him again. "And after that, we'll go take a look at the old Masterson place. I've got a feeling it's going to play a major role in our future."

Epilogue

One year later

Mattie Meadows-Vance propped her hands on her hips and stared at her husband. "I can't believe I let the judge talk me into an open house. I'm not ready, Denver. The house isn't ready. And everyone in McCray County is due in less than two hours."

Denver walked up beside his wife of six months and wrapped an arm around her waist. "Stop worrying so much, sweetheart. You know your mom and all the other McCray ladies, not to mention your Vance relatives, will be here any minute to help with the finishing touches. And the house is beautiful, just as we knew it would be."

Mattie sagged against him. "I suppose you're right. Beth Ann assured me that she and Mom McCray will be bringing all the food."

"Right. Fortunately, Megan has agreed not to cook."

Mattie slapped her husband on the back. "Stop maligning poor Megan. She has the triplets to keep her busy. She doesn't have time to cook."

"Hey," Denver objected. "I knew her before she had children. She couldn't cook then either. Besides, she's my niece so I can talk about her if I want to."

Mattie grinned. She knew Denver was trying to take her mind off the upcoming open house, but she couldn't be distracted for long. Her adoptive parents and siblings were coming up from Georgia, and the entire town of Barbourville, not to mention everybody in McCray County, had been invited.

The judge had assured her that not everyone they'd invited would come, but she'd noticed that he'd cleared off the five-acre field beside the house in case they needed it for parking.

"At least Dogwood winter is behind us," she said. "I was so afraid that the cold spell wouldn't end by today."

"The judge told you to stop worrying about it, that today would be warm and fair. When are you going to stop doubting him?"

"About the time he stops trying to interfere with our lives."

"You love his interference, and you know it. After all, he's just trying to be a father to you."

"Well, I hope he's gotten over that ridiculous notion that I should drop the Meadows name and start calling myself Mattie Kessler-Vance. It's not that I don't respect my real father's memory, but I'd never do anything to hurt my adoptive parents."

"I think you can stop worrying about that, sweetheart. And speaking of the judge, isn't that his pickup turning onto the lane?"

"Looks like it. I wonder why he's coming so early."

"Maybe he's bringing Evelyn."

"No, because she wouldn't have agreed to haul the food in the back of a pickup truck."

"True," Denver said. "Look, he's stopped at the end of the driveway and is letting the tailgate down. We'd better go investigate."

"We sure had." Mattie sighed. "No telling what he's up to now."

Ten minutes later, Mattie stood at the foot of the driveway leading to her and Denver's home and bit back a smile while she stared at the beautiful wrought iron sign the judge and Denver were setting into place on the side of the drive.

In large letters arranged in a semicircle over an ornate flower resembling a dogwood blossom were the words MEADOWS-VANCE HOUSE.

"It's my housewarming present for the two of you," the judge announced, stepping back to admire his gift. "I'm tired of everybody referring to this as *the old Masterson place.* It's got new owners and it deserves a new name. Of course I really would have preferred—"

"It's great," Denver interrupted quickly. "In fact, it's perfect, just the way it is. Thanks, Judge McCray."

The judge grinned, then glanced at Mattie's still very trim waistline. "It's the least I could do. After all, if my grandbabies are going to have the last name of Meadows-Vance, I want everybody in the county to be very familiar with it before the little ones start coming along."

Mattie closed her eyes and struggled for control for a few seconds before giving in and laughing out loud. She might have the most interfering stepfather in the country, but he was also the most original.

And she understood that when she and Denver got around to starting a family, their children would always possess a secure knowledge of who they were and where they came from.

If nothing else, the judge would see to that.

She smiled at her stepfather and then stood on tiptoe to plant a kiss on his cheek. "I love it. And with your gift to show people the way, I'm sure this will be one of the most enjoyable housewarmings McCray County has ever seen."

The judge grinned. "It will be *the* best, my dear. You can bet on that. Now let's go on up to the Meadows-Vance House and open the door because I see my precious wife turning onto the lane and she's going to need help carrying all that food into the house."

The judge climbed back into his truck and pulled up the driveway, leaving Mattie and Denver alone to admire their new sign.

Denver wrapped an arm around Mattie's shoulders. "Any regrets, my love?"

She rested her head against him for a few seconds. "No regrets," she said. "Just the opposite in fact. I first came to Barbourville looking for my mother, and I found not only her but an extended family and, best of all, you."

Denver planted a kiss on the side of her head. "Speaking of your mother, we'd better get out of the center of the driveway before she runs us over."

They stepped to one side and were standing beside the MEADOWS-VANCE HOUSE sign when Evelyn McCray turned onto the driveway and, with a quick toot of her horn, greeted them as she passed by.

Then Mattie and Denver walked side by side up the driveway to their new home and their future together.

CPSIA information can be obtained at www.ICGtesting.com
Printed in the USA
LVOW101608070512

280698LV00011B/94/P